The
Redemption of
Oscar Wolf

Also by James Bartleman

As Long as the Rivers Flow (2011)

Raisin Wine (2008)

Rollercoaster: My Hectic Years as Jean Chrétien's Diplomatic Advisor 1994–1998 (2005)

Out of Muskoka (2004)

On Six Continents: A Life in Canada's Foreign Service (2004)

The Redemption of Oscar Wolf

JAMES BARTLEMAN

DUNDURN
A J. PATRICK BOYER BOOK
TORONTO

Editor: Allison Hirst
Design: Jesse Hooper
Printer: Friesens

Library and Archives Canada Cataloguing in Publication

Bartleman, James, 1939-
    The redemption of Oscar Wolf / by James Bartleman.

Also issued in electronic format.
ISBN 978-1-4597-0982-9

    I. Title.

PS8603.A783R43 2013   C813'.6   C2012-906546-3

1 2 3 4 5   17 16 15 14 13

 Conseil des Arts du Canada Canada Council for the Arts   Canada   ONTARIO ARTS COUNCIL CONSEIL DES ARTS DE L'ONTARIO

We acknowledge the support of the **Canada Council for the Arts** and the **Ontario Arts Council** for our publishing program. We also acknowledge the financial support of the **Government of Canada** through the **Canada Book Fund** and **Livres Canada Books**, and the **Government of Ontario** through the **Ontario Book Publishing Tax Credit** and the **Ontario Media Development Corporation**.

Printed and bound in Canada.

VISIT US AT
Dundurn.com | Definingcanada.ca | @dundurnpress | Facebook.com/dundurnpress

Dundurn	Gazelle Book Services Limited	Dundurn
3 Church Street, Suite 500	White Cross Mills	2250 Military Road
Toronto, Ontario, Canada	High Town, Lancaster, England	Tonawanda, NY
M5E 1M2	L41 4XS	U.S.A. 14150

For my mother, Maureen Benson Simcoe Bartleman,
a member of the Chippewas of Rama First Nation who was born
in Muskoka in 1922 and spent her summers at the
Indian Camp in Port Carling as a child.

Contents

Author's Note

From the early to mid-twentieth century, the period covered in this book, Canadian indigenous persons usually described themselves as Indians or Natives. Today, we refer to ourselves variously as Aboriginal persons, First Nations persons, Native Canadians, Natives, Indians, or by our national and tribal identities such as Chippewa or Ojibwa. Many of us no longer use the term *Indian* because in the past some non-Natives employed it in a derogatory or racist manner. Likewise, in the timeframe of the novel, Australian indigenous persons generally described themselves as Aborigines. Today, many prefer to be called Aboriginal persons or by their regional names such as Koori, Murri, and Nunga. I use the terms *Indian, Native, Chippewa, Ojibwa,* and *Aborigine* as appropriate to reflect the historical context of the novel.

This book is a work of fiction. With the exception of members of my family, any resemblance between the characters and individuals, living or dead, is entirely coincidental. Port Carling is a composite creation, based only in part on the village of that name. The fictional village incorporates physical features taken from other small communities that dot Canada's Precambrian Shield country. The attitudes of its inhabitants toward Native people are an amalgam of attitudes prevalent in mainstream Canadian society prior to and after the Second World War. In recent years, the real village of Port Carling has emerged as a place whose people maintain close and welcoming ties of friendship with their Native neighbours and community members.

Cast of Characters

Oscar's Family

Oscar Wolf: the protagonist

Stella Musquedo Wolf: Oscar's mother

Jacob Musquedo: Stella's father; Oscar's grandfather

Louisa Loon Musquedo: Jacob's wife; Oscar's grandmother

Caleb and Betsy Loon: Louisa's parents; Oscar's great-grandparents

Amos Wolf: Oscar's father, killed in action in the Great War

Rosa Morning Star: Oscar's wife

The Others

Clem McCrum: village drunk, Port Carling

James McCrum: Clem's father and prominent local businessman

Leila McTavish McCrum: Clem's mother

Reginald and Wilma McCrum: Clem's grandparents, Muskoka pioneers

Reverend Lloyd Huxley: minister of Port Carling Presbyterian Church

Isabel Huxley: wife of Reverend Huxley

Claire Fitzgibbon: tourist from "Millionaires' Row," Muskoka

Dwight and Hilda Fitzgibbon: Claire's parents

Harold Winston White: Claire's husband

Mary Waabooz (Old Mary): Chippewa elder

Gloria Sunderland: the butcher shop owner's daughter

Georges Leroux: Canadian ambassador to Colombia

Pilar Lopez y Ordonez: receptionist, Canadian embassy, Bogota

Luigi Ponti: anthropologist, Colombia

Robart Evans: Canadian high commissioner to Australia

Ruth Oxley: secretary to High Commissioner Evans

Reverend Gregory Mortimer: chairman, Australian Royal Commission on the Status of Aborigine Peoples (ARCSAP)

Father Adrian Murphy: member of ARCSAP

Captain Mary Fletcher: member of ARCSAP

Anna Kumquat: Australian prostitute

Larry Happlebee: deputy minister of Indian Affairs

Stuart Henderson: Canadian ambassador to South Africa

Bishop Jonathan Tumbula: Anglican bishop of Soweto

Joseph McCaully: minister of External Affairs

Sergeant Greg Penny: Ontario Provincial Police

Chief Zebadiah Mukwah: Osnaburgh Indian Reserve

The Creator, the old people used to say, put tricksters like you on Mother Earth so he could have a good laugh at your expense from time to time.

— BETSY LOON TO OSCAR WOLF, SEPTEMBER 1935

Prologue

1914 TO 1917

1

The afternoon newspapers had reported that thousands of Canadians had been killed and wounded at the Battle of the Somme, and the mood of the people of Toronto was grim on that hot and humid September evening of 1916. Streetcar operators clanged their bells angrily at the cars and trucks ahead of them in the traffic, and drivers in turn honked their horns impatiently at defiant jaywalkers. Men and women out for an evening stroll to escape the oppressive heat of their apartments and houses were quick to take offence, shoving back when jostled, however accidentally, by other pedestrians.

Stella Musquedo, a tall and muscular Chippewa teenager, who looked much older than her sixteen years, with dark-brown skin, piercing coal-black eyes, and straight raven-black hair, walked through the crowds, oblivious to the mood of the others. Married against her will just two months earlier to a soldier she barely knew who had shipped out to the trenches of northwestern France a few weeks later, she had just learned she was pregnant. But the last thing she had ever wanted was to bring a child into the world who would suffer as she had suffered from the lack of parental love, and she wanted to end the pregnancy as soon as possible. She had made an appointment with a doctor who was prepared to break the law to perform an abortion, and was on her way to see him.

❖

Stella's earliest memory of Mom dated back to one summer when she was four or five. It was early morning and she was camping with Mom and Dad on an island somewhere near the Indian Camp. Dad had caught a fish, and even though it was gooey, she had helped him scale and clean it, cut it into pieces, roll them in flour, and drop them into a frying pan of sizzling lard over the fire. Mom, as usual, had let them have all the fun.

After they ate, Dad took the canoe and went back out fishing. It was such a beautiful day. There were big white clouds in the blue sky and seagulls and crows were circling, looking for some scraps to eat. It was so hot, and Stella wanted to go splash in the water. There was no use asking Mom to take her. She would say no; she always said no. So Stella started walking toward the shore alone. There were bushes with blueberries on them, and she ate a few; they tasted so good. There was a little black and white bird sitting on branch singing, but it flew away as she approached.

When Stella reached the water she peered in and looked at all the pretty stones on the bottom. It didn't look deep at all, so she slid down on her stomach into the water. But it was suddenly over her head and she was choking. Stella scratched at the rock with her fingernails until she managed to pull herself out. She looked up, there was Mom looking down, smiling at her as if she really wasn't there. Mom had been watching the whole time but had not helped her. That was when Stella knew Mom did not love her; Mom wanted her dead.

When Stella was six, Mom died. She cried for a little while because she thought that was what everyone wanted her to do. Dad lifted her up onto his knees and told her he had met Mom many years before when he had a job way up north. She had come south to marry him but had had a hard life away from her family. He said he missed her a lot, and he knew how much Stella must miss her as well. But she didn't really; Mom had wanted her dead.

Stella became really worried when Dad told her he was sending her to residential school because he couldn't take care of her anymore. But he told her that the white people there would teach her all sorts of useful things. So she helped Dad pack her clothes and they walked hand in hand along the dusty reserve road to the railway station early one morning.

The train arrived in a lot of smoke and noise and confusion and they got on board. The seat was made of some sort of cloth but was so hard and itchy that Stella got up and stood at the open window looking out at the trees, houses, and barns that rushed by. The rocking of the passenger car and the clickety-clack of the wheels on the track made her sleepy, but the smoke and ashes pouring in the window made her cough and kept her awake. Another train went slamming by, going the other way. She cried out and stepped back in fright and Dad laughed, lifted her up beside him on the seat, and told her there was nothing to be afraid of.

Dad bought her a chocolate bar and a bottle of pop and pointed out things to her as they went along — cows and horses and cars, things like that. Dad had never been that nice to her before and Stella was really happy. She went back to the window and watched the sun race behind the telephone poles and yet never move. She thought of Mom who was dead and felt guilty for not being sorry. She thought of Dad who was still alive but who would grow old someday. She wanted Dad to be like the sun racing behind the telephone poles, but never changing and never dying and making her feel sad.

It wasn't fun anymore when they got off the train. It was dark and she was tired. A man was waiting for them at the station and he took them in a car to a big building where there were lots of lights burning. She went in with Dad and the man, and everyone was friendly, but when she turned around to say something to Dad, he was gone. He had left her alone with a lot of strangers.

Someone took her someplace and cut off her braids and shaved her head. Someone else poured coal oil on her naked skull and it stung. Another person gave her new clothes to put on. After she had something to eat, Stella went to bed. That's when she got real homesick and started to cry. She missed Dad a lot and didn't understand why he had left her. She told herself he'd be back in the morning, but when he didn't come back, she knew he had never loved her either. He had just been pretending when he had been nice to her on the train.

❖

Stella did not see her father again for ten years. Every June at the end of the school year the other children left to pass the summers with their families, returning when school started again after Labour Day. Each year, Stella would spend the summer at the school together with a few other children who either had no homes to go to or who were unwanted by their families. For the first few summers she was disappointed, but each time he did not appear, she made excuses to herself for his behaviour: He had been attacked and beaten up by burglars. He had slipped and broken a leg. He didn't have the money for the train fare.

As she grew older, however, and her father still didn't come for her, her disappointment turned to desperation and then to anger. She blamed her mother for dying and her father for leaving her in the hands of people who beat her for coming late to class, who asked her to their offices to touch her private parts and in return to reveal their private parts to her, who made her work long hours cleaning floors and scrubbing pots and pans, who fed her slop hardly fit for animals to eat, and who allowed the big kids to bully the small ones.

As more years passed, her anger turned to a deep feeling of betrayal and bitterness. No one ever said she loved her, held her when she was upset, or took her hand when she was sick. To the staff, Stella was just one of hundreds of Indian inmates to be fed, watered, and educated in the ways of the white man until they were released back into their communities like prisoners who had served their terms. By the age of thirteen, Stella was bullying the smaller students as she had been bullied. By the age of fourteen, with her wide hips, large breasts, and a loud laugh, she radiated an animal magnetism that attracted grown men and rendered adult women uneasy in her presence. By the time she was fifteen, she decided she would not let her father get away with leaving her in such a place, and wrote him a letter:

May 30, 1915

Dear Dad,

I am your daughter and you haven't been nice to me. You took me to the school when I was six and forgot about me. I am now fifteen. The people here have been mean to me. Beatings, lots of awful things. I guess you don't care otherwise you would not have left me in such a place. The others get to go home for the summers. You forgot me. You never came although I used to wait for you. I remember going to our place at the Indian Camp in Muskoka

*in the summers and the fun I had there playing in
the water with the other kids when I was a little
girl. You are responsible for me aren't you? If so,
come and get me on June 30 when school is out
and let me have some fun this summer. I'll be outside on the steps with my things. Please don't let
me down!*

Your daughter,
Stella

P.S. Don't forget to come. It's not too much to ask.

On the last day of the school year, Stella waited outside on the
school steps with the other students going home for the summer,
but her father did not come. She had had enough. She would make
him sorry and teach a lesson to all those people who had mistreated
her over the years. She would go to Toronto and make her own
way in the world. She got to her feet, left the bag with her clothes
behind, exited the school grounds, and began walking south on the
gravel highway.

A car pulled up beside her and the driver rolled down the
window, stuck his head out and said "Want a lift?" Stella opened
the door and climbed in.

"Running away from school?" the driver, a middle-aged
white man wearing a white short-sleeved shirt and tie, asked her.
His jacket was lying on the back seat.

When Stella didn't answer, he said, "I thought so, but don't
worry, I won't tell on you. How do you like my jalopy?" he asked,
putting his car in gear and continuing down the road. "Just
bought it," he said, patting the dashboard. "It's a brand new Model
T Roadster, the only one in this neck of the woods. It's my car and
I can do anything I want with it. My wife has her own, but it's not

a Roadster: she uses it to drive the kids around and go shopping. And to show you I'm a fine fellow, in addition to letting you ride in my brand new fancy car, I'm going to share a drink with you."

Stella took the already opened bottle of gin that he held out to her, raised it to her lips, and drank deeply. It was the first time she had tasted alcohol, and it burned her throat. But it was good. She took another long drink and that was better. She took a third, longer drink and that was even better.

"Hey, slow down, that's all the booze I got in the car," he said, yanking the bottle from her hands and drinking from it until there was no gin left. Stella leaned back in the seat and closed her eyes, her head spinning. A few minutes later, she felt the car turn off the highway and she opened her eyes as the white man drove up a gravel driveway and parked in front of a house secluded in a dense grove of poplar trees.

"This is the old homestead," he said, turning and smiling at her. "Want to come in and look around? Maybe have a bite to eat and a glass of lemonade before you hit the road again? What do you say?"

Stella nodded her assent, opened the car door, and, although unsteady on her feet, followed the chattering white man up the walkway.

"You're really lucky you ran into me," he said, taking out a key, unlocking the door, and holding it open as she went in. "The police keep a sharp eye out for runaways on that stretch of road. You wouldn't have got far before they caught you. How old are you anyway? Eighteen? Nineteen? I thought they let you kids go home for good when you turned sixteen. But I guess they make exceptions for exceptional students. Now just make yourself at home while I make us something to eat," he said, steering her into the living room and telling her to take a seat on a sofa.

"I make good sandwiches. Want one?

"I see you're a little shy," he said when Stella did not respond. "I don't blame you. You probably think I invited you in to take advantage of you. But I'm not like that. I'm a respectable insurance agent who goes to church regularly and follows the Golden Rule in everything: *Do unto others as you would want others to do unto you.* That's been my motto since my Sunday school days. Now please excuse me, while I see what there is in the icebox," he said, grinning at her as if he was privy to some secret joke.

A minute later, he reappeared with a glass of lemonade mixed with gin and thrust it at her. "Here, drink this while I whip up some lunch. There's nothing in it that'll do you any harm."

Ten minutes later, he reappeared with a platter of tomato and lettuce sandwiches, cold, peeled hard-boiled eggs, and a pitcher of lemonade into which he had poured a half bottle of gin. He sat down beside her.

"Help yourself to the food and some more lemonade," he said, reaching over and patting her on the knee. "You must be hungry and thirsty after spending time out there in the sun."

Not having had anything to eat or drink since early that morning, Stella eagerly ate and drank while the white man kept his eyes on her, smiling indulgently.

"My wife, kids, and dog have been away for the past week at the cottage. I get really lonely when they're not here. Family is really important, don't you think?" he asked, pouring her another gin and lemonade and edging up against her. "Do you have brothers and sisters?" he added, inserting a hand between her legs. Stella removed his hand and pushed him away. The white man leaned back, took a sip of his drink, and pointed at a series of framed photos in which he and a middle-aged woman were sitting smiling in deck chairs on a beach with two happy teenagers posing behind them.

"That's me, the little woman, and the kids," he said. "I'm so blessed to have such a great family. I don't know what I would do without them."

❖

A half-hour later, Stella came to lying on a bed with her clothes off and her new friend on top of her doing his best to rape her.

"Come on, Pocahontas," he was shouting. "I know you like it!"

Stella shoved him aside and sat up, confused and wondering where she was and how she had come to be on this strange bed. And who was this naked white man beside her?

He slapped her, and she remembered getting into a car, drinking alcohol straight from a bottle, becoming dizzy, and being hungry and eating and drinking while this white man tried to fondle her and droned on and on about his wonderful family.

She slapped him back. But she did not stop at slapping him back. She was bigger than he was, and she got off the bed, turned around, and, fueled by the alcohol and years of pent-up rage, she hit him as hard as she could in the face with her fist. As blood gushed from his nose, splattering the sheets, she jerked him onto the floor and kicked him repeatedly in the stomach and groin. Leaving him curled up and moaning, she proceeded to trash his house, hurling to the floor the framed photographs the white man had just shown her, pitching cups, saucers, and dinner plates against the walls, throwing heavy glass ashtrays through the windows, and opening the ice box and emptying bottles of milk and cream, tomatoes, cucumbers and lettuce, slabs of butter, and cartons of eggs onto the floor.

After retrieving her clothes and dressing, Stella left the house, went down the driveway to the highway, and carried on walking south toward Toronto. Whenever a car stopped to offer a lift, she waved it on, unwilling to repeat her encounter with the crazy white man. An hour later a car drove up behind her and she turned around, ready to tell the driver to keep on going. But this time it was a police cruiser.

"Come over here and let me have a look at you," the cop said, leaning out the window.

Stella obeyed his order, afraid the white man had reported her to the police for beating him up and making a mess of his house. Instead, he asked her if she was Stella Musquedo from the residential school. When she confirmed her identity, he told her to get in.

"The principal of your school is worried about you," he said. "He asked us to track you down and bring you back."

Inside the cruiser, the cop's mood changed when he smelled gin on Stella's breath. "Don't you know it's against the law for Indians to drink? For minors to drink? For bootleggers to sell to Indians?"

"No one sold anything to me. It's just your imagination."

"Don't give me any of your lip. I'm going to tell the school that you've been into the booze and they'll deal with you."

Stella didn't care. The worst she would get would be ten lashes of a belt across the bare legs and she had received that many times before. But once back at the school and being led by a hectoring teacher to the basement to receive her punishment, she once again decided that she had had enough. She shouldered the teacher aside and walked slowly up the stairs, defying him to try to stop her, and left the building. This time, to avoid meeting the cop who had delivered her to the school, she made her way to the railway tracks where a locomotive with a load of boxcars was beginning to pull out of a siding. One of the doors was open, and as she ran toward it, a half-dozen hobos standing inside waved and yelled at her to come join them. She reached up and they hauled her inside and welcomed her to their world. After sharing a bottle of cheap wine with her, they told her their hard luck stories and gave her tips on how to survive in the big city.

"You being an Indian and all that, you won't have a chance in hell of getting any sort of job. You're going to have to use your wits to survive, bumming spare change on the streets and knocking on doors for handouts."

"The Salvation Army's always good for a meal and place to spend the night if nothing better turns up. But you gotta close your eyes and be polite when they pray for your soul."

"When I was on the bum in Quebec," another hobo said, "I used to go looking for monasteries when I was hungry. The monks were always good for an apple and a sandwich. But you had to get there early in the morning before they ran out."

❖

Stella jumped off the train when it slowed to a crawl approaching the freight yards in downtown Toronto. She had no friends, no money, no knowledge of the city, and she had a splitting headache. But she was free for the first time in her life to do whatever she wanted.

A hard-faced railway cop carrying a truncheon told her to get a move on. "I seen you get off that train. If I ever see you here again, it'll be the Don Jail for you."

"Go to hell, you asshole," she said, and ran off when he came after her. She stopped a passerby to say she was hungry and to ask where she could find a monastery or the Salvation Army.

"Don't know any monasteries around here. But the Salvation Army's got a soup kitchen over on Jarvis Street and it's not a long walk."

The soup kitchen was closed when Stella reached it and she stood at the door waiting for it to open, asking people for spare change. Eventually, someone came out and told her to go away and come back later. She then noticed that there were women, their faces powdered and their lips smeared with lipstick, standing on the sidewalk beckoning to men in uniform. Although raised in a residential school, Stella knew they were whores. A teacher at the school had once tried to humiliate her by calling her that when she asked for money after he had sex with her, but it hadn't bothered her. One of the women saw her and came over.

"New in town?"

"Just arrived on a freight. Don't know anyone down here."

"What's this about a freight? Did you really just arrive in town?" A pimp had been listening to the conversation, and over a coke and a hamburger he told Stella that he could help her make a lot of money.

"I'll provide you with a room to do your work and spend your free time, and I'll be around to protect you if the johns cause trouble. You're young and the customers like that. But you're an Indian and a lot of guys around here don't like Indians. Just the same, the city's been full of lonely soldiers since the start of the war and they'll pay one dollar for every trick you turn. My cut is fifty cents. Interested?"

❖

One September evening, fifteen months later, Stella was standing on the sidewalk on Jarvis Street outside the King's Arms Hotel, which rented rooms by the hour to prostitutes to carry out their business. One of her friends, a big, raw-boned Ojibwa teenager from a reserve in northern Ontario, who had likewise drifted onto the streets after running away from her residential school, was with her. The two women were doing what they did every day at that time: trying to catch the eyes of potential customers cruising down the street in their cars. But it was hot and muggy and business was slow. A car stopped, and the driver leaned out the window and motioned to Stella to come over to him. But as Stella began to discuss prices, the other woman pushed her aside and took her place.

"Goddamn Indian bitch," Stella hissed, grabbing her by the hair, dragging her away from the car and pushing her down on the pavement.

"Goddamn Indian whore," the other girl replied, scratching Stella's face and pulling her down on top of her and kneeing her in the groin.

"The cops!" someone yelled.

The john drove quickly away, the crowd dispersed, and the women ran up the steps into the hotel. Shortly afterward, Stella's father, Jacob Musquedo, entered the hotel and spoke to the clerk behind the desk.

"I've been told Stella Musquedo lives here," he said. "I need to talk to her."

"You a cop?" the clerk asked. "I guess not," he said, glancing at Jacob's dark brown face and not waiting for an answer. "Wait right here and I'll go get her. She just came in in a bit of a hurry."

A few minutes later, a smiling Stella, her face swollen and scratched, came down the stairs.

"Looking for a good time, handsome?" she said, not recognizing her father. "I give special rates for Indians and extra special ones for old men like you."

"Stella? Are you Stella Musquedo? Can we go up to your room? I've got something to say to you."

2

Shortly after the start of the Great War in 1914, well before Jacob found his daughter working the streets of Toronto, a recruitment officer addressed a public meeting at the Chippewas of Rama Indian Reserve. "Our country is in peril," he told the assembled people. "Tens of thousands of young Canadians have already fallen in battle in Europe fighting alongside their British cousins under the leadership of His Majesty King George V whose grandmother, Queen Victoria, was the beloved mother and protector of all the Indians of Canada. Men are needed to replace them as soon as possible, for the hour is late and the Hun is winning."

With his unlined face and raven-black hair, Jacob looked decades younger than his actual age of fifty-one, and had no difficulty in persuading the recruitment officer to let him join up. In May of the following year, he received Stella's letter pleading for him to let her go home for the summer, but set it aside after reading it, just as he had with the others she had sent him over the years. Ignoring his daughter's correspondence, in his way of thinking, however, did not in any way mean that he was unmoved by her pleas for help. His overriding desire was to do what was in her best interest, and in his opinion she was better off staying at the residential school in the safe hands of its staff than spending the summer at the Indian Camp where she would probably start running around with the boys. And as for her complaints of mistreatment by her caregivers, he simply did not believe her. It would have been a waste of time to write to tell her what she already knew anyway.

Nevertheless, he began to worry about what might happen to his daughter if he were to be killed in action, finally deciding to marry her off as soon as she turned sixteen to a suitable Chippewa man who could take care of her if that should happen. All the eligible bachelors from the reserve, however, had joined up and were as much at risk of being killed as he was. After much reflection, he came to the conclusion that if his daughter were to marry someone who was killed in action, she would at least receive a pension. And so in the coming year, Jacob studied the young recruits from his reserve doing their basic training with him to find the best possible husband for his daughter. Eventually he settled on Amos Wolf, a hard-working young man of twenty whose elderly parents had passed away when he was still a teenager.

"I need someone to write to when I'm overseas," Amos told Jacob, who cultivated him as a friend and mentor. "What if I get killed? Just look at the casualty figures. Who'll remember me when I'm gone? I've no one left at home and I'd really like to have a family before I die, maybe a son to carry on my name."

At first Jacob listened with fatherly indulgence as Amos spoke of his fears and hopes. He nodded his head sympathetically when Amos told him in the strictest confidence that although everyone thought he was outgoing and happy-go-lucky, he had always been shy around girls.

"I don't know how to talk to them" he said. "They make me feel inadequate. I never get up the nerve to ask anybody out."

Then one day in early June 1916, Jacob let slip that he had a daughter just a bit younger than Amos.

"Her name is Stella. After her mother died, I couldn't take care of her and she's been away for years at a good residential school learning to read and write and cook and sew and be a good wife for the right man. I'm going to get her at the end of the month and she'll be home to stay after that. If you want, I could put in a word for you."

Amos asked people on the reserve who had known Stella before she went away to residential school for their opinion.

"Haven't heard of her for years," was the general view. "Her mother was a strange, lost soul who died when her daughter was just a child. No idea what she's like now, but if she takes after her father, she's sure to be hard-working and reliable."

Later that same month, about to be shipped out to Europe to join his regiment on the front lines, Jacob managed to get family leave. He arrived at the residential school dressed in his military uniform to bring his daughter home to meet Amos.

"She left last summer and didn't come back," the principal said when Jacob asked for her.

"What do you mean, 'left and didn't come back'?" asked Jacob. "Was she in some sort of trouble?"

"Well, you may not like what I've got to say," the principal said. "She was a model student the first years she was here, but she never received mail from home and she spent her summers at the school rather than with her family. I am afraid she thought you had rejected her and she started to take her frustrations out on the other students and the staff. Matters came to a head last year when she was under the impression you were coming to bring her home for the summer. When you didn't appear, she left the property without permission and we had to send the police to bring her back. She left again and we thought she had gone home. The police came later to say she had somehow entered someone's home, trashed it, and attacked the owner. We never followed up, thinking it was for the best since we couldn't handle her and she would have been charged with assault had she returned."

"Where do you think she went?" Jacob asked. "I've got to find her and I don't have much time before I go overseas."

"Why don't you try Toronto," the principal suggested. "A lot of our female runaways hitchhike or ride boxcars down there and try to find jobs as maids, waitresses, or babysitters. The problem is Toronto is such a big place, it'll be hard to locate her."

❖

But finding Stella was all too easy. When Jacob visited the downtown police station to file a missing person's report, the cop on duty asked him to wait while he went to look for her name in the files in the registry.

"Your daughter is not missing, Mr. Musquedo," he said when he came back. "In fact, she's well known to us. We've had to bring her in for fighting, disturbing the peace, public drunkenness, and for soliciting on the streets. She moves around a lot but the last address we have for her is room 10, the King's Arms Hotel, on Jarvis Street next to the Salvation Army soup kitchen."

"Thank you, thank you just the same," Jacob answered, not knowing what to say. "I'm leaving for overseas in a couple of weeks," he told the cop who was no longer listening.

I should have brought her home for the summers, Jacob thought, as he walked toward Jarvis Street. *I should have done something when I got her letter last year. Maybe she wouldn't have disgraced herself and the family. Maybe there was nothing I could have done to help her anyhow. Nobody can blame me. I did what I thought was right for her, just like I'm doing for Canada by going off to war. Luckily, I've found a good man for her.*

3

After the initial shock of meeting her father, Stella did not try to hide her disbelief when Jacob said he wanted her to come home with him and settle down before he went overseas.

"You're a cold old goat," she said. "You never wanted me when I was a kid, and now to make yourself feel good, you come around pretending you care about me. So go away and let me live my life as I want. Toronto's my home now, not the reserve or the Indian Camp. The women selling their asses on the streets, including that bitch I was just fighting with, are my family, not you."

Two days later, however, Stella pushed open the door to Jacob's house on the reserve and walked in carrying her suitcase. "Don't look so surprised," she said to her father who was eating his dinner. "You knew the cops would come looking for me after the fight and I'd have to come back to the reserve to hide out for a while."

The next day, Jacob invited Amos Wolf to drop by for a cup of tea. And Amos, who had been so well prepared by Jacob that he had already fallen in love with the idea of marrying his daughter before he met her, could not have been happier when he was exposed to her earthy humour, handsome good looks, and worldly self-confidence. There was no need, Jacob thought, to tell him that he had found Stella working the streets of Toronto. Why spoil his illusions when he might well be killed overseas anyway?

At the request of Amos, Jacob told his daughter that his friend wanted to marry her, but she said no.

"Why this sudden concern for me?" she asked. "There's gotta be something in it for you."

"Not at all," said Jacob. "I just want what's best for you. Besides, the government will send you half his pay when he's overseas, and if he gets killed you'll get a pension."

❖

Within a week, Stella and Amos were man and wife. Within two weeks, Jacob and the bridegroom left to rejoin their regiment and go overseas. Two months later, Stella was sitting in the office of the helpful doctor who was telling her that for a substantial fee he would get rid of her baby. But although she still didn't want a child, she couldn't bring herself to go through with the abortion. Seven months later, Oscar was born, and four months after the birth of his son, Amos was killed in action during the battle for Hill 70 near the town of Lens in northwestern France. It was August 1917.

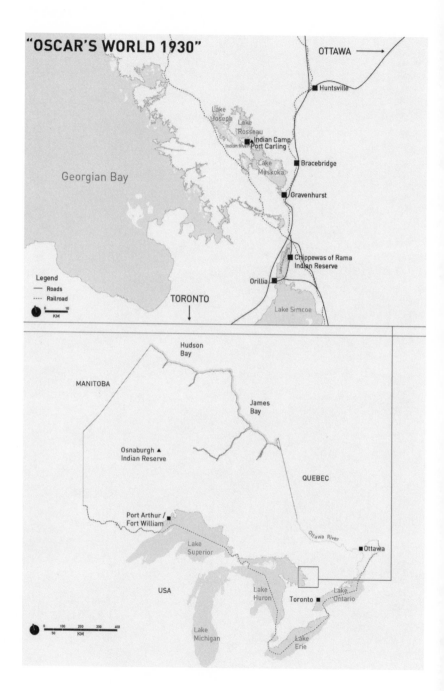

"OSCAR'S WORLD 1930"

OTTAWA →

Huntsville

Lake
Joseph
Lake
Rosseau
Indian Camp
Indian River Port Carling

Georgian Bay

Lake
Muskoka
Bracebridge

Gravenhurst

Legend
— Roads
---- Railroad

0   10
KM

Chippewas of Rama
Indian Reserve

Orillia

TORONTO
↓

Lake Simcoe

Hudson
Bay

MANITOBA

James
Bay

Osnaburgh ▲
Indian Reserve

QUEBEC

Port Arthur /
Fort William

Ottawa River

Ottawa

Lake
Superior

USA

Lake
Huron

Toronto ■

Lake
Ontario

0   100   200   300   400
50
KM

Lake
Michigan

Lake
Erie

PART 1

APRIL TO JUNE 1930

Chapter 1

THE JOURNEY

1

Mary Waabooz, lovingly known as Old Mary to her friends and relatives, the oldest member of the Rama Indian Reserve, had died, and the people crowded into her modest house late in the evening were singing the reassuring old gospel hymns in the language of their ancestors. The light of a solitary coal-oil lamp at the head of the open coffin threw a shadow down over her body, softening the gaunt features of her face, making her look decades younger and bringing a look of peace to someone who had spent the last weeks of her life in agony. It did the same for the other old people in the room, ironing out the creases on their foreheads, erasing the wrinkles on their dark brown, leathery cheeks, and concealing the slack flesh on their necks. There was a smell of decay mixed with sweetgrass in the room. The mood was one of calm and acceptance. There was no weeping. Old Mary had outlived three husbands and two grown children and her time had come. And yet her death still hurt. It was like an ancient tree, a landmark in the history of the community, unexpectedly crashing to the ground, leaving a massive empty space in the lives of the people.

Jacob Musquedo, his hair as black as ever despite his sixty-seven years, sat quietly near the door, anxious to leave. Stella, who had grown into a massive middle-aged woman of some two hundred and fifty pounds and who had prepared the body for burial earlier in the day, stared morosely at the flame of the lamp. Only Oscar, now thirteen years old, his hair pulled back and twisted into one thick black braid and with black watchful eyes set in his dark, high-cheek-boned face, sang along with the others. He was there mainly because he wanted to be close to his mother whom he loved but who did not love him. He was also there because he had been a friend of Old Mary and had often gone to her house on winter evenings to eat hot fried bannock, to drink tea with sugar and condensed milk, and to listen to her talk about the world of her youth.

"When I was a little girl," she used to say, "we believed in Giche Manitou, the Creator, and not in the God of the Christians. We believed in Madji Manitou, the evil spirit, and not in the devil of the Christians. We believed that all things, animals, stones, water, and everything visible and invisible possessed souls, just as humans did. We believed that a monstrous seven-headed serpent with eyes the size of dinner plates inhabited the lakes of the Chippewa homeland in Muskoka. We believed that Mother Earth was Turtle Island and that it had come into being from a grain of sand carried by a muskrat to the surface of the sea without beginning or end. We believed that the Milky Way was the handle of a bucket holding up Turtle Island. We believed that the first humans emerged from the dead bodies of animals and were first cousins of the animals."

Oscar always felt a tremor of fear run down his spine when Old Mary's eyes began to glisten and she went on to tell tales of witches, shape-shifting bearwalkers, cannibalistic Windigos, and other evil beings that owed their allegiance to Madji Manitou and who roamed the Earth doing harm to humans. He much preferred her accounts of the battles his people had fought over the years. He became a war chief when they drove the invading Iroquois from their hunting grounds; he became Pontiac when Chippewa warriors captured British fort after British fort at the end of the Seven Years' War; he was at the side of his great-grandfather fighting the Americans in the War of 1812; and he was with his father and grandfather fighting the Germans in the Great War. In every one of these engagements, he saw himself as the hero battling impossible odds to impress his mother and gain her admiration and affection.

❖

At eleven-thirty, Jacob signalled to Oscar that it was time to depart, and grandfather and grandson went around the room, taking their leave of the mourners sitting in chairs pushed back against the walls. But Stella, when they came to her, refused to take their outstretched hands and looked away. They murmured their goodbyes anyway and went quietly to the door, picked up their packs, left the property, and started down the gravel road to the railway station.

Suddenly, a half-dozen dogs burst out into the starlight from behind a house and ran barking toward them, but they fled whimpering back into the darkness when Jacob picked up a rock and hurled it in their direction. His seasonal job as a handyman at the McCrum and Son Guest House at the Muskoka village of Port Carling, close to his summer home at the Indian Camp, started the next morning at eight o'clock. He and Oscar needed to catch the midnight train to Muskoka Wharf Station at Gravenhurst at the bottom of Lake Muskoka and paddle throughout the night if he was to report for work on time. James McCrum, the proprietor, wouldn't care whether or not there was a death in the family or a pack of dogs blocking his way and would probably fire him if he was late.

Thirty minutes later, they smelled the creosote of railway ties and off in the distance heard the shriek of a steam whistle. Quickening their pace, they reached the station just before the locomotive, shaking the rails and pulling two dozen passenger and freight cars, its headlight cutting a path through the night, came thundering around the curve of Lake Couchiching. It had left Toronto four hours earlier and was on time.

With a hiss of air brakes, a cloud of coal smoke, grease, and soot, the train came to a jerking stop. The door at the rear of a coach opened and the conductor, a lantern in his hand, peered out into the gloom in search of passengers. He kicked down the stairs when he saw Jacob and Oscar standing on the platform.

"Tickets, please," he said, when they came aboard, holding out his hand to take and punch them. "It's dark in here," he whispered as he lighted the way with his lantern and led them into an over-heated coach filled with sleeping passengers and reeking of sweat, stale food, and cigarette smoke. Coming to two empty places, he said, "These should suit you fellows. Stow your gear on the racks above your heads. You'll be getting off at the next stop."

Oscar took the seat closest to the window and sat silently in his separate world as the locomotive, panting with enormous gasps of steam like some primeval dragon preparing for combat, its driving rods pounding and its giant wheels straining as they turned, pulled out of the station. Scraping a peephole in the frost covering the inside of the window, Oscar looked out at the starlit countryside as the train picked up speed and hastened forward at sixty miles an hour. He thought back to the wake, to the single mesmerizing coal-oil lamp casting its soft light over Old Mary's body and the elders in the room who had seen and done so much in their long lives.

What had the old people been thinking? Were they recalling the days when Old Mary was young and they were young? Remembering the days when the families had returned from their winter hunting and trapping grounds in the spring to spend the summers together at the Narrows where Lake Simcoe emptied into Lake Couchiching? The days when they would talk about births and deaths and finding the perfect person to marry? The days when the ancestors undertook spirit quests, when they gathered sweetgrass for ceremonies, and when they held community feasts? Or, as they looked at Old Mary in her plain pine coffin, were they mourning the loss of their youth and counting the days until his mother appeared at *their* homes to wash *their* dead bodies and put *them* on display in plain pine coffins in *their* living rooms?

And what meaning did Old Mary's death have for him, for Oscar Wolf, his head pressed against the window staring out through the opening in the frost as the train raced through railway crossings empty of traffic, its wheels clicking ever more rapidly on the rails, and its whistle wailing? He was sad because Old Mary had been his friend and was now no more. But at the same time, for some unexplainable reason, her death made him feel more alive than ever and astonished at the wonder of existence.

"You owe your birth to blind luck," Jacob once told him when he was a little boy, "since your parents knew each other for only two weeks before your father went overseas and was killed."

Oscar at first had accepted his grandfather's judgement, but as he grew older and started to think for himself, he came to the conclusion that luck had nothing to do with it. Divine Providence was the cause. In contrast to Old Mary, perhaps because he regularly attended church, he believed in the Christian God as well as the Native Creator and felt their presence when he said his prayers before he went to bed and at church during Sunday services. They had put him on Mother Earth for a purpose, he was sure.

And although that purpose would only be revealed in the fullness of time, he liked to think he was destined to do great things for his people someday. Maybe he would be a great warrior like Tecumseh, who rallied Indian warriors from across Canada and the United States to save Canada from the Americans in the War of 1812, only to die in the process. Or perhaps like John Brown, the white American who gave his life at the Battle of Harper's Ferry trying to free the slaves. Maybe, like Tecumseh and Brown, he would sacrifice his life for a great cause someday. Maybe then his mother would treat him with the respect other kids got from their moms.

Oscar wished his father was alive and he could discuss his thoughts with him. But he had been just a baby when his father was killed and he knew him only from his framed black-and-white picture, in which he sat smiling at the photographer and seemed so happy to be wearing the dress uniform of the 48th Highlanders of Canada. The photograph hung in their house back on the reserve, beside one of Jacob wearing a similar uniform. Oscar often looked at that picture, trying to decide what sort of man his father had been. Lots of his father's friends from the old days had told him stories of going hunting and fishing with him. How he used to run away laughing at the white game wardens when they tried to catch him. He was a throwback to the old Chippewas, they said, someone who could control his canoe in the most dangerous rapids, someone who was a crack shot, someone who never got lost in the bush, and someone who knew and respected the old ways. Everyone said he had a bad temper and once had got so mad at the Indian agent, whom he had caught trying to cheat the people, that he threw him down the stairs of the band office and broke one of his legs. The RCMP had hauled him up before a judge and he spent six months in jail.

Jacob told him his father had died a hero when the Canadian Corps launched an attack on the Germans entrenched on Hill 70 in northern France in August 1917. When he was old enough,

Oscar checked out a history of the Great War from the library and read and reread the account of the battle until he practically had it memorized. Although he was proud of his father's war record, he hated the Canadian government for sending him to his death and depriving him of a dad as he grew up. For as long as he could remember, he had wondered whether his father knew he was going to be killed when the picture was taken. Did he think of the newborn son he had never seen when he was dying? Did he regret he would never be able to take him fishing and hunting and do all the things fathers usually did with their sons? Was he sorry he would never be able to help his people before he died?

2

The train slowed to a crawl, moved across a bridge spanning the gorge over the Severn River, which flowed northwesterly out of Lake Couchiching into Georgian Bay, and climbed laboriously up a steep grade to enter the District of Muskoka. Twenty minutes later, Oscar and his grandfather were standing on the deserted platform at Muskoka Wharf Station as the sound of the train, with its load of passengers bound for Bracebridge and Huntsville and places farther north such as Timmins and the twin cities of Fort William and Port Arthur, faded away. Nearby, they could hear the groans of the steamers of the Muskoka Navigation Company rubbing their bumpers against government docks as they waited for the beginning of the tourist season and the arrival of day trippers from Toronto.

A minor official of the navigation company, a returned soldier who had served under Jacob in the war after he had been promoted on the battlefield to the rank of sergeant, had given his old army buddy permission to leave his canoe on the covered wharf over the winter. After confirming it had suffered no damage, Jacob and

Oscar picked it up and slid it into the black water. They then took their positions, grandson in the bow and grandfather in the stern with their packsacks between them on the floor, and began their journey to the Indian Camp. There was no wind, but the ice had been off the lake for only a week; the night-time April temperature was well below freezing and each breath of air chilled their lungs. If all went well, they would be at their destination in six hours.

As Oscar paddled, the words and melodies of the hymns sung around the coffin earlier that night played over and over in his mind. At first he found them distracting, preventing him from concentrating on the things he wanted to think about on this special night on the water. But he soon gave in and sang aloud the words of his favourite hymn.

> *Shall we gather at the river,*
> *Where bright angel-feet have trod,*
> *With its crystal tide for ever,*
> *Flowing by the throne of God.*
> *Yes, we'll gather at the river,*
> *The beautiful, the beautiful river,*
> *Gather with the saints at the river,*
> *That flows by the throne of God.*
> *On the margin of the river,*
> *Washing up its silvery spray,*
> *We will walk and worship ever,*
> *All the happy, golden day.*

As Oscar sang, tears of exultation flooded his eyes and he became conscious of the presence of someone, of something otherworldly, and he looked up at the stars and saw the outline of a smiling face. Old Mary, he recalled, had once said that the old people believed that humans were composed of three parts: a body that rots in the dirt after death; a shadow that watches over the grave of the corpse as well as the members of the dead person's family and closest friends; and a soul that travels westward over the Milky Way to reside in the Land of the Spirits. The Land of the Spirits, she said, was ruled over by Nanibush, the right hand and messenger of the Creator, whose power ran through all things.

It's Old Mary, he thought. *Her shadow followed me here from the wake, and now her soul on its final journey is watching over me as I sing out here on the lake in the middle of the night. And the soul of my father,* Oscar remembered, *travelled on that same road to the Land of the Spirits after he was killed in France.*

Oscar sang louder, shouting out the words of the hymn to the starlit sky.

3

Oscar's passionate singing irritated Jacob, but he said nothing. If his grandson found some comfort from attending church and singing Christian hymns, good for him. Personally, he found their messages of love and forgiveness, if you were lucky enough to be counted among the chosen, hypocritical. His service in northern France as a soldier had led him to equate Christianity with cities in rubble, the suffering of civilians, and the massacre of soldiers. A lukewarm Christian before he went overseas, he had returned with a renewed attachment to the Indian beliefs he had embraced as a boy and abandoned as a man many years before. Like many other things in his life, he kept his beliefs to himself.

Puffing hard on his pipe, Jacob thought of the disrespect his daughter had shown to him and to Oscar at the wake. He was not angry — becoming upset would do no good — but he was worried about her. When he had come back from the war, neighbours on the reserve had told him that in the years he had been away, Stella did not seem to care for anyone or anything. She drank, she ran around with any low-class white man who took her fancy, often disappearing for weeks at a time, leaving her baby with Old Mary to look after. She would return smelling of alcohol, her hair a mess and her body covered in bruises when she had run out of money and needed to cash her pension cheques. She laughed too loud, they said, and she became involved in brawls whether she was sober or drunk. She was unpredictable; no one knew what would set her off. She was more than willing to take on anyone in a fight, man or woman, old or young, big or small, with fists, feet, and fingernails; a piece of cordwood would do if she was losing. She was, they said, just plain crazy.

Jacob suspected the neighbours might well be right. At the turn of the century, he and three other men from the Rama Reserve were working for two white men from Toronto, surveying the hunting and trapping territories of the Ojibwa people who lived on the headwaters of the Albany River, deep in the northwestern Ontario bush. One morning, a birchbark canoe paddled by a Native glided toward them out of the early morning mist.

"Bojo, Bojo," the visitor, who spoke their language, called out to the men on the shore eating their breakfast. "Do you think the white men would give me work? I was born here and know the best fishing spots."

The man was in his early sixties with a thick salt-and-pepper moustache, broad shoulders, a massive chest, and thick, powerful arms. He had taken the trouble, Jacob saw, to apply for work with his shoulder-length hair neatly cropped and he was dressed in what were probably his best clothes: black fedora, knee-high buckskin moccasins decorated with coloured beads and porcupine quills, a bandanna knotted around his neck, and a shirt loosely tucked into pants held in place by a red and white sash.

"We're not here to fish. But come ashore and have something to eat with us and then I'll go ask them if they can use you."

"Tell him he can start right away," the white men said when Jacob passed on the request. "We can use someone who knows the local landmarks."

Jacob quickly made friends with the stranger, whose name was Caleb Loon, and passed the summer working alongside him by day and spending his evenings with him and his family. He enjoyed Caleb's company and liked his wife, Betsy, a large, dark-skinned, heavy-set, good-humoured woman in her early thirties who was invariably dressed in a plain calico dress pulled over a pair of men's pants and knee-high moccasins. He was happiest in the company of their daughter, Louisa, who was big-boned and tall like her mother and already a woman at the age of sixteen. She spent the evenings staring inscrutably into the fire as if she was thinking about matters so profound that she could never share them with anyone. While obviously too young for him, she was exactly the sort of girl he had always wanted to marry. Good looking when the flickering light of the campfire shone on her solemn face, she was, in his view, just like one of those unspoiled and unsullied Indian maidens who lived at the time of the ancestors.

Caleb and Betsy noticed Jacob's interest in Louisa and questioned him closely about the life of his people in the south. They found it most interesting when he said most people owned their own houses on his reserve and spent their summers at the Indian Camp on the shore of a river in Muskoka where their kids swam and played in the water while their parents made good money selling handicraft and fish to rich white people. They were most attentive when he told them that he was still a bachelor at the age of thirty-seven.

"That's not old," Betsy said, smiling at Jacob. "I was only fifteen when I accepted Caleb's marriage offer and changed my last name from Amick to Loon. And he's thirty years my senior. It was the same with my parents. My father's first wife had died and he was over fifty and my mother was sixteen when they got married. And it was a good marriage."

By summer's end, it was understood that Jacob would wed Louisa. The day after the first frost of the season, Betsy simply informed him that her daughter would marry him before they returned to their winter trapping grounds in the fall. Two weeks later, the members of the survey party ended their work for the season and returned to the railway station and from there by train to their homes in the south. Three weeks later, Louisa arrived at the railway station at the Rama Indian Reserve, and one week later she married Jacob.

It would not be a happy marriage. Jacob had mistaken damage for dignity and shyness. He would never discover that the decade Louisa had spent at residential school had crushed her spirit. From the age of six to sixteen, she had listened to teachers say that Indians had been godless savages before the arrival of the white man, and their ancestors, not having heard the Word of the Lord, were burning in Hell. She had been forbidden to speak her Indian language, her name had been replaced by a number, and she had been beaten by the nuns and sexually abused by the priests. She returned to her parents traumatized, having lost her culture and knowledge of life in the bush and knowing only a few words of Ojibwa. Her parents had been anxious to find a husband who could take care of her as soon as possible.

The summer after her marriage, Louisa gave birth to Stella in Jacob's shack at the Indian Camp, and until her death six years later, she rejected her daughter. At first the other women thought she was just suffering with the sort of melancholy new mothers sometimes have after the birth of a baby but usually shake off after a few weeks. But when months, and then years went by, and Louisa continued to neglect Stella, they knew something was fundamentally wrong. And when she went to bed one day, turned her face to the wall, and starved herself to death, no one was really surprised.

When he came home from the war, therefore, and learned of his daughter's erratic behaviour, Jacob concluded that she had probably inherited the mental illness that had cut short the life of her mother. He thus made allowances and tried to shield her from herself by chasing away predatory white men whenever he could. His protective instinct extended to her little boy, and he intervened when he found Stella beating him. She once threw Oscar outside naked into the snow, paying no attention to his screams, and it was just good luck that he happened to arrive home at that moment to bring his grandson inside.

When he told his daughter she had to change her ways, she just laughed at him. "I didn't want that kid when he was born and I don't want him now. If you love him so much, why don't you just take him off my hands and raise him yourself."

Jacob had sought to do just that, but it was not easy. He had no wife to help him, had no special parenting skills, and found it no easier to establish intimate ties with his grandson than he had with his own daughter. Perhaps that was the reason he made Oscar call him Jacob rather than grandpa or even grandfather. To make it worse, Stella was living in his house and it was heartbreaking to see her constantly shoving her little boy away when he was just trying to show her his love. He did what he could, making sure Oscar ate regularly and buying him decent clothes. When he was old enough, he sent him to the day school on the reserve where the white teachers, although hard on the kids, were at least teaching them some reading, writing, arithmetic, and other skills needed to survive in the white man's world.

To shield him as much as he could from the influence of his mother, Jacob took Oscar out of the school on the reserve each spring when he started work at the guest house and let him attend classes at the school for white kids at Port Carling.

Oscar was now set to graduate from elementary school at the end of June, and since there was no high school on the reserve, he would have to leave at the end of the summer and attend a residential school until he was sixteen. And although his daughter had nothing good to say about the residential school she had gone to, maybe that was just because girls were more apt to become homesick than boys. Oscar would do okay.

4

A fierce wind from the northwest plains that had crossed Lake Huron and Georgian Bay and swept up and over the leafless highlands now came howling down onto the lake, whipping the water into rows upon rows of white-capped breakers that pushed the canoe off course. Oscar stopped singing as he and Jacob fought their way to a protected passageway between a large island and the shore.

For the next hour they paddled through a wide channel lined with oversized boathouses. Great steamer docks proudly adorned with sixty-foot-high flagpoles, their ropes rattling in the wind, protruded aggressively a hundred feet out into the water. Behind the docks, scarcely visible in the starlight, were wide walkways leading up past tennis courts and wide lawns to huge summer houses with upper-floor balconies and wraparound verandas. This was Millionaires' Row, the preserve of the American and Canadian super-rich whose parents and grandparents had visited the district to hunt and fish in the late nineteenth century. It was still a land of poor bush farmers then and they were able to buy up the shorefront they needed at a cheap price to recreate the country-club life they enjoyed at home.

The waves were as high as ever when they left the shelter of the channel, but the wind was now at their backs and they began to make up for lost time. The cold, however, cut through Oscar's clothes and his teeth began to chatter.

"Lie down on the floor and cover yourself with blanket," Jacob told him. "I'll wake you up when we reach the manido."

Sometime later, a splash of cold water coming over the gunnels struck Oscar in the face. He woke up to see, in the grainy light of the predawn, the head of a blind chief emerging from the rock on the north-facing outcrop of a deserted island alongside that of a smaller inert guardian companion. As ancient as Turtle Island itself, its face was covered in lichen, its cheekbones were fractured and its nose broken. Inscrutable, it exuded profound sadness and complete indifference to the waves crashing against its base and to travellers who came to pay it homage. The old people said it was, in fact, the Creator himself in another form.

Taking hold of his paddle, Oscar held the canoe as steady as he could in the seething waters, freeing Jacob to light his pipe, and with his arms and hands outstretched, raise it into the air and offer a prayer to the unsmiling deity.

"Oh Great Manido, I beg you to protect two humble Chippewa canoeists from the wrath of the seven-headed water snake that dwells in the depths of this lake. I beseech you to allow us to travel in peace and safety to the Indian Camp. And bring us good luck, Oh Great Manido, as we try to catch a fish for our breakfast on this last leg of our journey."

He then blew an offering of smoke to the statue and told his grandson to fish while he paddled. Oscar pulled the gear from a pack — an eight-inch silver spoon armed with triple gang hooks at the end of three hundred feet of thirty-pound test copper trolling wire — and fed it slowly into the water until it was only a few feet from the bottom. He gave the line a jerk, making the spoon leap forward, and a fish immediately took the bait. Oscar hauled in the line, hand over hand, keeping tension on the wire to keep it from breaking free. Jacob turned the bow of the canoe into the wind and held the boat steady until his grandson pulled the fish, a two-pound lake trout, over the side.

Jacob murmured a prayer of thanks to the Manido for answering his appeal and, clenching his pipe in his teeth, steered toward the mouth of the Indian River, a mile away. The final and most emotionally wrenching part of his journey was about to begin, for he was coming home to a place that no longer existed. He was coming home to Obagawanung, known as Indian Gardens by the first settlers. He had been born there in 1863, son of the chief and grandson of a veteran of the War of 1812 who had left the Rama Indian Reserve in the 1840s to look for a place where his family could live in peace away from the white man's whiskey and religion. The veteran had found such a spot in the middle of the traditional hunting grounds of his people in a place so rocky and unfit for farming and with weather so harsh that he thought white men would never want to settle there. A dozen other war veterans and their families joined him and they built their village just below the rapids at the headwaters of the Indian River, six miles upstream from where it fed into Lake Muskoka.

5

Jacob had treasured Obagawanung when he was a child. It was a holy place where Mother Earth was most alive, where the people were part of the world around them, where the manidos were everywhere in the surrounding lakes and rivers and in the trees, the rocks, the animals, the fish, the clouds, the lightning, and the passing seasons. In the winters, he used go outside at night to listen to them whisper to each another in the mist that rose up from the current. In the spring, he would wait eagerly for the annual visit of the half-breed traders who came from their posts on Georgian Bay in birchbark canoes laden with guns, ammunition, and other supplies to exchange for beaver, muskrat, and wolf pelts. In the summers, he camped on an island in Lake Muskoka picking blueberries with his family, and in the autumns he went hunting with the men for deer and bear. He thought he would spend the rest of his life at Obagawanung, but one day when he was five or six, white men came and surveyed the lands, and the settlers arrived soon after.

Now, only half a dozen rotting log cabin homes, used as pig-pens by the farmer son of one of the first settlers, remained of that world. With one exception, the graves of the inhabitants had been picked over by archaeologists seeking specimens of so-called primitive man to put on display in museums or ploughed into the ground by settlers years ago, leaving the shadows of the dead to wander without a home. The grave that was spared was that of Jacob's grandfather, who had died of grief when told by the Indian agent that his people would have to abandon their homes to make way for the immigrants in search of land coming from across the Great Waters.

In bitter memories that he had shared only with his grand-son, Jacob remembered, as if it were just yesterday, helping his father and the other men of the condemned community take his grandfather's body one moonless night, when no white people were watching, and bury it at the mouth of the river at a secret place on a high point of land overlooking the Manido of the Lake. At that time, there had been no sign of human life anywhere in this part of Lake Muskoka. Now, six decades later, a gazebo had been constructed over the grave and shuttered summer cottages occupied building sites every two or three hundred feet along the indented and rocky shore.

Not long afterward, the police came with rifles and told the people they had to go, and they loaded whatever they could carry in their birchbark canoes and departed. Most would leave for a reserve on a rocky island on Georgian Bay and a life of poverty, but a few, including Jacob and his family, went to the Rama Indian Reserve seventy miles to the south where they had family to help them.

Jacob never forgot the white people standing on the shore cheering their expulsion, nor the huge piles of logs and brush burning on both sides of the river as they paddled away. His father told him the white people were making the point to the Chippewas that they could never return to their homes, that their time was over and that the time of the settlers had come. It was of little comfort to Jacob that the government later created a tiny reserve called the Indian Camp where his people could spend their summer months within the boundaries of the newly incorporated white village of Port Carling. If anything, it made him feel worse, since each time he paddled by the site of his former home he was assailed by thoughts of what his life might have been like if only the white people had shown his people some compassion.

6

An hour later, the sun was up, the wind had died down, and the ground was white with hoar frost. As they rounded a bend in the river, the two paddlers smelled wood smoke in the air and off in the distance they had their first view of Port Carling, a cluster of clapboard houses on both sides of the river, their windows framed with white-lace curtains and their backyards filled with chicken coops, privies, and half-empty woodsheds.

Twenty minutes later, they paddled past the *Amick*, a steam-powered supply boat owned by Jacob's employer, James McCrum, moored to the government wharf. When the tourist season began, it would start its rounds delivering groceries, ice, and sundries to its well-off clients on the surrounding lakes. Up the hill, on the road leading off the bridge that spanned the Indian River, was the village business section, a row of one- and two-storey frame buildings with high false fronts to make them appear bigger than they were. On the other side of the bay, visible from the government wharf but cut off from the rest of the village by a ridge, were the two dozen one-room shacks of the Indian Camp where Oscar and his grandfather would spent the next six months.

A few minutes later, they pulled their canoe up onto the shore and Jacob took out a key to unlock the door to the shack he had built after he had married Louisa. The door, however, was ajar. Someone had entered over the winter months, but nothing, it seemed, had been stolen. The beds and mattresses, the linoleum-covered table pushed up against the window facing the lake, the chairs, the old cook stove, the pots and pans hanging from nails on the bare studs, the axe and saw, the woodbox, and the cutlery and crockery in the orange crates scavenged at the village dump and used as cupboards remained as they had been left the preceding fall. The smell of stale ashes, wood smoke, coal oil, and last year's fried fish meals hung in the air. Sunlight streamed in through the windows devoid of curtains and blinds, but the building was cold and damp.

Oscar followed his grandfather into the shack and quickly checked his precious collection of books, bought with the money he had earned in past summers washing windows and sweeping walkways at nearby tourist cottages. His copies of the lives of Tecumseh and John Brown, and his illustrated copies of *Swiss Family Robinson* and *Treasure Island* were still there, he saw to his relief. So, too, were the two used volumes of the 1911 *Encyclopedia Britannica* and his collection of books written by veterans on the Great War. Nothing had been touched. He pulled from the woodbox a copy of the *Toronto Star* dated August 1, 1929, its fading headlines still proclaiming "Stock Market Crash, Dozens Jump to Their Deaths on Wall Street," stuffed it into the stove, added dry kindling, and lit a fire.

Jacob returned to the canoe, retrieved the lake trout and cleaned and filleted it on the shore, tossing its guts to the seagulls that came swooping in, crying raucously to be fed. By the time he returned to the shack carrying the fillets, Oscar had unpacked the food supplies brought from the reserve and put the kettle on to boil. He picked up the heavy, fire-blackened cast iron frying pan that had been in the family for generations, placed it on the stove, scooped a big tablespoon of lard from its can, and spread it with his fingers over the cooking surface. While he was occupied with these tasks, Jacob rolled the fillets in flour and eased them into the lard that had started to boil and spit. Oscar quickly cut two boiled potatoes into slices and dropped them into the simmering mix. A short while later, grandfather and grandson, wearing their coats at the table, drank their tea and ate their breakfast in silence. Jacob then glanced at his pocket watch and left for the guest house, looking forward to meeting his friends from the village whom he had not seen since the previous fall.

"Don't worry about making dinner," he said as he went out the door, "I'll pick up a few things at the store and I'll see you when I get back from work."

Oscar finished his meal, washed the dishes, and took a seat by the window. In a few minutes, he would trudge up the hill through the snow on the north-facing ridge and go down the sun-lit slope on other side to the four-room combined elementary and high school, each with its separate entrance. The big boys from the high school would be standing just outside school property by the gate leading to their entrance, their shirt collars turned up against the cold. They would be shifting their weight from foot to foot, smoking roll-your-own cigarettes or chewing tobacco and spitting the wads on the ground as they waited for the bell to ring calling them to class. The big girls would already be inside their classrooms combing and brushing their hair, gossiping and organizing themselves for the day ahead.

In the playground of the elementary school, the girls would be skipping rope and chanting a rhyme they repeated endlessly at this time of the year.

Down by the river, down by the sea,
Johnny broke a bottle and blamed it on me.
I told ma, ma told pa,
Johnny got a spanking so ha ha ha.

The boys would be horsing around, playing marbles and kicking a soccer ball, but they would not invite Oscar to join in. He would go inside and ask the teacher if he could attend classes for the rest of term. The teacher would say yes, as he always did when Oscar appeared at his door at this time of year. He seemed to like Oscar, but, with a mocking smile never called him by his name, always addressing him as Chief. The kids called him Chief, as well, but never with a smile. To them, he was the outsider, even if most of them treated him with good-natured tolerance. Several others, big raw-boned members of an old pioneer family, however, called him a dirty Indian and had been bullying him for years. Once when he was a seven-year-old in grade two and fought back, they had ganged up on him, threw him to the ground, and pushed his face into the dirt.

"Say 'I'm a dirty Indian,'" they said, "and we'll let you go." But Oscar refused to give in, and his tormentors yanked him to his feet, and, as two of them held his arms, a third pulled down his pants to show off his underwear.

"Wanna see this Redskin's dick?" the older of the two asked the kids who had gathered around.

"I would," Gloria Sunderland, the butcher-shop owner's daughter said with a smirk. And after the big boys pulled down his underwear, Oscar ran back to the shack at the Indian Camp in tears to tell his grandfather what had happened. He expected Jacob would immediately go up to the school to tell those kids never to touch his grandson again or he would teach them a lesson they would never forget. And if their fathers got mad and came down to the Indian Camp to complain, his grandfather would pull *their* pants down to let them know how his grandson had felt when their sons had done that to him. After all, Jacob had killed Germans with his bare hands and was a war hero and had the medals to prove it. Dealing with the fathers of a couple of bullies in Port Carling shouldn't be all that hard.

But his grandfather took him by the hand and led him to the shore and sat down with him on a piece of driftwood. "I have seen and learned a lot of things in my life," he said. "To avoid torturing and poisoning myself with feelings of hatred, I banished from my heart the bitterness I once felt toward the people who expelled my people from Obagawanung. I discovered that the best way Indians can survive in the world of the white man is to fit in and wait for better days. I sent your mother to residential school so she would learn to fit in; I joined the army and fought the white man's war so I would fit in; and to fit in today, I smile and say nothing when youngsters half my age call me Chief at the guest house. That's why I think you should say nothing when the white children give you a hard time at school. Just remember: keep your heart free from anger, fit in, and wait for a better day and all will be well."

Oscar would never forget his grandfather's words, but as he grew older and listened to Old Mary's stories about the deeds of the ancestors in past wars, and to the veterans talking in the evenings around the campfires at the Indian Camp about their exploits in the Great War, he grew more and more ashamed of his grandfather for not coming to his defence. If his father were alive, Oscar was sure that he wouldn't have let anyone push his son around. And he vowed to get even, not just with the two white boys and Gloria Sunderland, but with everyone in the village, no matter how long it took.

Chapter 2

THE INDIAN CAMP

1

In the dark of the early morning before sunrise, Stella pushed open the door of the shack, stepped across the sill, and stood for a minute just inside, a lit cigarette dangling from her lips. Although she couldn't see her father and son in the black interior, she could hear their calm, regular breathing. Good! They were asleep, and if she was careful, they wouldn't wake up as she went to bed. Not that she cared what either one of them thought, especially Oscar, who would say nothing but stare at her reproachfully for coming in so late. Her father, however, would be sure to take her to task for spending the night drinking, and she didn't want to waste her time arguing with him.

But despite her best effort to cross the room to her bed quietly, she bumped into the cook stove and hurt her leg. Swearing softly under her breath, she bent over in pain before straightening up and hobbling over to the table in front of the window facing the bay and collapsing noisily into a chair.

"Are you all right?" asked Jacob, getting out of bed and lighting a coal-oil lamp.

"I don't want to talk about it," she said, stubbing out her cigarette in a saucer and massaging her aching leg.

"Looks like someone hit you a good one," he said, holding up the lamp and taking a close look at her. "It was Clem, wasn't it? That drunk was hanging around the Indian Camp all week until I told him to go away. He laughed like a madman as usual when caught in the wrong but he wandered off just the same."

"Leave me alone," she replied, taking another cigarette from its package and lighting it. "I don't need an old hypocrite like you to tell me how to live my life."

2

Just after supper the day before, Stella had arrived on the steamer from the reserve in a bad mood. Her breath smelled of wine and she was carrying two suitcases filled with beaded moccasins lined with rabbit fur, porcupine quill boxes, souvenir toy tomahawks, and miniature birchbark canoes to sell to the tourists over the summer. When Jacob asked her how Old Mary's family was coping after her death, she didn't bother to reply but sat impatiently chain-smoking cigarettes at the table, looking out the window across the bay. Oscar had then taken a seat beside her and quietly mentioned that he had beat out the class-brain and won a book as a prize for being top student in the graduating class at the Port Carling elementary school. But his hope that she might say something nice to him, or perhaps look at him with an approving smile, was not to be. Shrugging her shoulders and frowning, she had blown out a mouthful of smoke and resumed her vigil without even glancing at him. Finally, late in the evening when it was already dark, and after muttering to no one in particular that she had "something to do," she had gone out and headed up the path in the direction of the public wharf.

Oscar had slept fitfully throughout the ensuing night, bitten by the mosquitoes that came in through the screenless windows left open to provide some relief from the early summer heat, and worried that his mother would come to harm roaming around in the dark without her father or son to protect her. He now lay on his bed, his blanket pushed to one side, watching the shadows cast by the coal-oil lamp off the arguing adults flicker on the ceiling. His mother and grandfather were the two most important people in his life, and when they hurt each other, they made him feel that he was in some way responsible.

As he dressed on the shore, he thought of the way his mother had ignored him when he told her he had won the book prize. She must have known she was hurting his feelings but didn't care. But then again, he shouldn't have been surprised. She had been nasty to him for as long as he could remember, even though he always made a big effort to please her. He had often wondered why that was so. Sometimes he thought the death of his father had unhinged her mind and made her incapable of thinking straight. Other times, he suspected she somehow blamed him for his death. There were even times when he believed she still loved his father so much she was afraid to betray him by showing affection to her son. The possibilities were endless. The result was, however, that she drank too much and had affairs with men like Clem who beat her up.

❖

In fact, Stella loved her son in her own way but was unable to express her true feelings to him. And for that, she blamed her father for turning her into a hardened and coarse human being. She had never forgiven him for leaving her in a residential school when she was a child of six, for not coming to see her, for not letting her go home for the summers, and for not answering the letters she sent him. She blamed him for the beatings and rapes she suffered at the hands of her supposed caregivers, for turning her into a classroom bully, and for the assault she suffered at the hands of the passing motorist when she finally fled the school. She blamed him for making her turn to the streets for her living, for making her stand outside in snow, rain, and scorching heat, her face garishly painted, smiling grotesquely at men cruising by looking over the women as if they were sides of beef. She blamed him for making her haggle with the johns who wanted to pay her fifty cents rather than the going rate for her services. She blamed him for the hangovers that greeted her in the mornings after drinking into the night to forget. She blamed him for having to accommodate the crooked cops who demanded her services for nothing. And most of all she blamed him for inducing her to marry someone she scarcely knew by telling her she would get a widow's pension should he be killed in action.

But as much as she blamed her father for all the harm he had caused her, she blamed herself even more. Not long after the birth of Oscar, a sergeant in dress uniform accompanied by the local Presbyterian minister knocked at Jacob's house on the reserve and handed her a telegram. "His Majesty's Canadian government regrets to inform you," she read, "that your husband, Private First Class Amos Wolf, was killed in action somewhere in northwestern France on August 16, 1917. God save the King."

"Can I come in and pray with you for the soul of your husband," the minister asked. But Stella slammed the door in his face. Several weeks later, the postman brought a letter informing her that she would receive a pension for life. Rather than being happy, she felt dirty and was filled with guilt for profiting from her husband's death. Afterward, every time she looked at her baby, she saw herself in her son, and since she deserved to be hurt, he deserved to be hurt, and it was all she could do to prevent herself from picking him up and bashing him against a wall. Her attitude made no sense, but afraid of what she might do to him, she handed him over to Old Mary to look after as often as she could and went to Toronto to forget her troubles by drinking and partying with her old friends from the streets. It had been a relief when her father undertook to raise him for her.

3

Looking out across the bay, lost in thought, Oscar noticed in the moonlight the outline of the *Amick* moored to the government wharf. Clem was its captain, and as Oscar and everyone else in the village and the Indian Camp knew, he spent most of his free time drinking and carousing on board with his buddies.

That's how my mother got those bruises, Oscar thought. *Clem lured her on board, tempted her to drink too much, and beat her up in one of his drunken rages.*

A wave of anger swept over him. He thought of the bullies who pulled down his pants when he was a little boy and of Gloria Sunderland who laughed at him. He thought of the Canadian government that sent his father to his death and of the settlers who took Obagawanung from his grandfather and his people. He thought of the teachers and kids who called him Chief at school, of the white people who gave him no respect because he was an Indian, of his grandfather who wouldn't stand up for his rights and who just wanted to fit in, and above all he thought of Clem who had hurt his mother. He was thirteen, the age Old Mary said Chippewa boys became men and warriors in the old days. He was going to show the white people they couldn't push this warrior around any more!

But he had no idea how to get even. And so, remembering the account of the battle for Hill 70 which he had read about in the book on the Great War he had borrowed from the library, he substituted daydreaming for action. It was August 1917, and he was a sergeant of the 48th Highlanders of Canada in a trench on the front lines waiting to attack the Germans dug into Hill 70. If the Canadians could take the objective, the Allies would break through the enemy lines and win the war. The artillery barrage, which had been going on for hours softening up the enemy positions, came to an abrupt halt and the commanding officer signalled to Oscar to lead the charge. Oscar raised his rifle to signal the others to follow him and crawled up and over the top. There was a moment of silence, and then the enemy opened fire with everything it had: artillery, mortars, machine guns, pistols, rifles, and canisters of poison gas. Men were falling all over the place. Some were running in a panic into barbed wire entanglements. Others were being blown to pieces and body parts were raining down. But he, brave Sergeant Oscar Wolf, was plunging ahead heedless of the danger, anxious to take his revenge against the Canadian government for sending his father to his death, against the bullies who had pulled down his pants, against everyone who had ever called him Chief, and against Clem for being mean to his mother.

All at once, his way was blocked by fire coming from a German machine-gun nest raking no man's land, killing and wounding everyone in its path. To escape the deadly onslaught, he dove into a shell crater, sliding headfirst into a deep pool filled with decaying corpses. He rose to his feet and spit out the foul-tasting, putrid water and looked up to a scene from John McCrae's "Flanders's Fields," which they recited during Remembrance Day ceremonies at school every November 11. Birds were flying across a brilliant blue sky among puffs of smoke from exploding artillery shells, and yet all was quiet. But Oscar had no time to spare staring up toward the heavens. There was a battle going on and the Canadian Corps needed him.

He clawed his way up the muddy side of the crater, and as he peered out over the lip onto the battlefield, silence gave way to the crump of exploding shells and the rattle of machine-gun fire. The slaughter of Canadian soldiers continued unabated, and as he looked on in fear and anger he saw his father lying dead on the ground. But there was no time to mourn his loss. Unless he put the machine gun out of commission, the entire Canadian offensive would come to an end!

Oscar crawled out over the lip of the crater and rushed forward, his rifle in one hand and a grenade in the other. Bullets whizzed by his head. A German soldier poked his head over the top of the sandbags protecting the machine-gun nest and looked at him. It was Clem. Clem was the German soldier who had just killed his father. He would recognize his long, thin, sallow face, his pale blue eyes, his hair-filled nose, his scraggly beard, and his disgusting yellow teeth anywhere! He lifted his rifle and shot him through the heart. Clem fell backward into the emplacement, cursing the day he had beat up Oscar's mother, incurring the wrath of her son. Oscar lobbed the grenade in after him. There was blood and guts everywhere. Victory was assured, but he, Sergeant Oscar Wolf, the bravest of the brave, had been gravely wounded and would soon be dead.

4

A dog began to bark, jolting Oscar out of his fantasy world. Looking around, he hoped no one would come out from the nearby shacks to investigate. It would be hard to explain what he was doing outdoors at that hour when everyone else was in bed sleeping.

"Be quiet!" someone yelled, and the dog whimpered and was silent.

Maybe I should just go back to bed and let Jacob handle Clem, Oscar thought. *After all, I'm not a warrior like the ancestors who fought the Iroquois for control of hunting grounds in the old days. I'm not a soldier in the Canadian 48th Highlanders like my father was before he was killed. Besides, those wars are over; I'm just a thirteen-year-old kid from the Indian Camp mad at a whole bunch of people.*

But as he stared across the bay at the moonlit outline of the *Amick*, Oscar thought again of his mother and her laugh of ridicule when he told her about winning the book for being top student in the graduating class. He then thought of the bullies who had pulled down his pants and exposed his dick to Gloria Sunderland. That led him to think again of Clem, who his grandfather said had hurt his mother, and he shifted the anger he felt against his mother and the bullies to his already existing rage against Clem until he lost control of himself and decided to torch Clem's boat.

His mind made up, he went to the barrel where Jacob stored the family's coal oil supply, filled a two-gallon can to the top with the flammable liquid, made certain he had a pocketful of matches, and moved as fast as he could up the path from the Indian Camp to the gravel road leading to the government wharf. Although tall for his age, Oscar had not yet filled in, and he found the can heavy and awkward to carry. After going only a few dozen yards along the path, the wire handle began to cut into his hand, rendering it numb, and when the pain shot up his arm, he stopped, hoisted his burden up to his chest, locked his arms around it, and kept on going. Coal oil slopped out of the open spout, splashing against his shirt, soaking it, irritating the skin of his chest, dripping down onto his pants and running down his legs.

❖

As he ran, Oscar returned to the world of his imagination, and he was no longer a kid bent on getting his revenge. He was Pegamegabow, the Ojibwa soldier from the nearby Parry Island Indian Reserve on Georgian Bay, the most decorated Native soldier of the Great War and hero to Native people everywhere for killing more than three hundred enemy soldiers with his sniper rifle. He was rushing up through a tunnel of overhanging tree branches on a mission to destroy an enemy machine-gun nest hidden in a floating grocery store moored to the government wharf. He had been shot in the chest and blood was gushing out of a painful open wound, wetting his shirt, soaking his pants, running down his legs, and dripping on the ground. No matter, he would carry on, whatever the odds.

A few minutes later, Oscar was standing at the top of the ridge that divided the Indian Camp from the white village, examining the lay of the land. Below him, in his imagination, was a German bunker in the shape of a supply boat occupied by members of the German army. That was his objective and he would destroy it. After lowering the can to the ground, he knelt beside it to catch his breath and to slow down his pounding heart. He rose to his feet and, keeping as low a profile as possible to avoid detection in the moonlight, half dragged, half carried the oil can across the bridge to the wharf and set it down on the planks some fifty feet from his target. Leaving it behind, he crept up to the boat like a Chippewa warrior in the old days sneaking up on the enemy.

There was a light coming from a porthole. Peeping inside, he saw German soldiers sitting around a table playing cards and drinking beer. From time to time, a German who looked like Clem said something that made the others laugh. Oscar was sure Clem was telling the others about beating up his mother and laughing about it and that made him all the more furious.

But he would have to change his plans. Setting fire to the boat was now out the question since the Germans would catch him before he could complete the job and turn him over to the constable. He decided to burn down the general store instead. That would teach Clem a lesson since it was owned by his father, James McCrum.

Oscar began to have doubts about his project as he was carrying his burden from the wharf to the business section. And by the time he slipped into the shadows under a ground-floor window at the back of the general store, he was crying. White people had done bad things, but what he was about to do was just as bad, maybe even worse. And what if he was found out? He would be sent to jail.

Fighting his fears, Oscar dashed around the general store, checking to see if there was anyone about. All was quiet, and he returned to his place in the shadows. To make doubly sure, he left again, this time running along the lane behind the guest house, the butcher shop, the Bank of Nova Scotia, the hardware store, and the furniture and casket shop. There was no sign of life. He scuttled down the boardwalk in front of the buildings. There was still no one around and he had a free hand.

He returned to his spot behind the store, waited a minute to catch his breath, and set off again, this time in search of a scrap of lumber to pry open the window. But he couldn't find anything to do the job. Getting down on his hands and knees, he felt around in the dark on the gravel laneway and came up with a handful of big stones that he hurled at the window, shattering it on impact and startling himself in the process. After waiting a few minutes to be sure no one was coming to investigate, he lifted the can up to chest level and rammed it through the broken window. Once again, the crash and clatter of breaking glass caught him by surprise, but this time he didn't hesitate. He lit a match and threw it into the opening. A flash of light revealed the can lying on its side with coal oil pulsating out of the spout and flowing out across the wooden floor.

The match spluttered and died. He lit another one and threw it inside but it met the same end, as did a succession of others that flickered and drowned in the liquid fuel before the oil could ignite. Something was needed to hold a flame long enough to cause combustion. He scurried around to the front of the store and rummaged through a garbage can until he found a week-old copy of the *Toronto Daily Telegram*. He dashed back, crumpled a page into a loose ball, set it alight, and pushed it through the window. This time the coal oil began to burn.

Not waiting to see if the fire would spread to the supplies stored in the room, Oscar lurched to his feet and ran for the safety of the shack as fast as he could. At the entrance to the path to the Indian Camp, he stopped, suddenly afraid of entering the dark tunnel. What if Clem, his friends, and the constable had heard the sound of breaking glass and were lying in wait for him? What if a bearwalker was hiding on an overhanging branch, ready to jump on him and steal his soul? What if a witch was to materialize and consume him in a ball of fire? What if the devil was to spring up and carry him off to hell?

And so what if they were! He had had the guts to get even with everyone who had ever hurt him and his mother and his people! He stepped into the dark confidently, only to hear the snap of dead branch on the path under his foot. In a panic, he plunged down into the black pit and ran as he had never run before, only to trip over a root in the dark and nose-dive to the ground. He struggled to his feet, his face bruised and bloody, and dashed ahead again recklessly in terror. He veered off the path into a tangle of chest-high ferns and burdocks, stumps of long dead and fallen trees, low-hanging branches, and sharp-thorn blackberry brambles that scratched his arms and legs. After thrashing around wildly in the dark for minutes that seemed like hours, Oscar stumbled back to the path, lost his footing again, and fell down, skinning his knees and elbows. He crawled, he scrambled, he limped, and he blubbered in fright, imagining that he was being pursued by all manner of monsters, eager to claim him as one of their own after the evil he had done that night. He pushed himself ahead as fast as he could, but his legs were leaden, his arms were frozen, his breath was laboured, and his body was drenched in sweat. He thought he would never reach home.

5

Panting from fear and exhaustion, Oscar threw open the door of the shack and stepped inside. Jacob and Stella looked at him through a fog of cigarette smoke.

"What are you doing out of bed at this time of night?" asked his mother, her words slurred, irritated that a third party had interrupted her never-ending quarrel with her father. "Come over here and let me have a look at you."

As Oscar approached, she grabbed his arm and slapped his face, bringing tears to his eyes.

"That's for not being in bed when I came in."

She slapped him again, this time harder.

"That's for not being here when I needed you tonight after I drank a little too much with Clem and tripped in the dark and hurt myself."

"Leave him alone," said Jacob. "He was here when you came in and went out for a walk. He's a good boy."

"Oh, no he isn't," his mother said, staring with glassy eyes at her son. "Nobody goes out for walks this late at night unless he's up to no good. He looks like he's been in a fight and he stinks of coal oil. What have you been doing anyway? Stealing something? I wouldn't put it past you."

She swung at him again, but this time he ducked.

"And stop looking at me like that, you little bastard. You want me to give you more of the same?"

Oscar jerked his arm free, stumbled to the door, and ran outside, his face stinging. It wasn't Clem's fault after all! He started running in a panic back up the path toward the village to put out the fire, but soon slowed down and stopped. He'd seen the flames spreading across the floor, and at that very moment they were probably consuming the building from the inside. He turned and walked slowly back to the shack, but hesitated at the door, afraid to go in and face his mother again. He heard the loud voices of his mother and grandfather through the open windows.

"I don't know what you got against Clem, but he's a good man," he heard his mother say to Jacob.

"If you knew him like I do you wouldn't think that," Jacob replied. "I've known him since he was a little boy when he spent his time spearing frogs and tormenting dogs and cats. I served with him overseas and know for a fact that he was a yellow-bellied coward and ran away from the fighting. He wasn't a real man and a hero like Amos."

"Clem's twice the man Amos ever was," Stella said. "Marrying him was the worst mistake I ever made. I never should have listened to you."

Oscar flinched, shocked that his mother would say such a thing about his father. Not wanting to hear her next revelation, he went to the shore and stood at the water's edge, his eyes full of tears, not knowing what to do next. Without warning, the bells of the Anglican church on the ridge overlooking the Indian Camp began to clang, jarring the silence of the night. The bells of the Presbyterian church answered from a hilltop elsewhere in the village and were soon joined by those of the United church, all delivering angry, cacophonic messages of impending tragedy, telling the people that some evil, foreign presence was abroad setting fires in their beloved community. On Sunday mornings, the three sets of bells conveyed coordinated messages of Christian charity and harmony as they called the faithful to worship. Now they echoed harshly, frantically throughout the village and up and down the river, summoning every able-bodied man and boy within earshot to rise from their beds and rush to fight the common enemy.

Then, off in the distance, Oscar saw a glimmer of light that grew in power until it rivalled the moon in its intensity. The bells continued to peal, now calling, now shouting, now announcing to the world that he, Oscar Wolf, thirteen-year-old Chippewa youth from the Rama Indian Reserve, who had just been honoured by the school principal with a book prize for being the grade eight student with the highest marks of the graduating class at the Port Carling elementary school, had done wrong and had disgraced the memory of his father. They declared to all that slinking around in the night and setting fire to the property of hard-working, innocent people was the work of an outlaw and a thief. They told him that no Native warrior or Canadian soldier would have stooped to such cowardly acts.

Overcome with the impact of his mother's revelation of her feelings about his father, unable to bear the wickedness of his actions, and afraid the constable was already coming to arrest him, Oscar waded fully clothed into the river. He hoped the water would swallow him up, make his problems disappear and take him somewhere where he could start his life all over again. When the water reached his chest, he stopped and looked back at the yellow light of the coal-oil lamp flickering on the pane of the shack's front window. Perhaps his mother or grandfather would come out and tell him he was just having a bad dream. When no one came out, he dove deep down into the dark waters of the bay and began swimming under the water and away from the shore, his eyes open but seeing nothing. When he could hold his breath no longer, he rose to the surface and swam farther and farther out away from the shore.

Chapter 3

THE FIRE

1

James and Leila McCrum were not unduly alarmed when they heard the fire bells of the three churches pealing before dawn that Sunday morning. Hotels around the lakes were always burning down, and there was little anyone could do about it. A guest would fall asleep with a lit cigarette or pipe, and the first thing you knew the tinder-dry wood building would be on fire. If there was time, someone would crank the telephone to appeal for help from the party-line operator on duty at the telephone office in Port Carling. She would call around until she found someone to go to one of the churches to pull the rope that rang the fire bell, which, as everyone in the village knew, was the shorter of the two that hung in the foyer; the longer one was to call the people to worship. The members of the volunteer fire brigade would assemble in front of the town hall, the Fire Chief would brief them, and everyone would crowd into cars and trucks and leave to fight the fire.

Since the firemen only had axes, shovels, and buckets as equipment, and since it took sometimes more than an hour over poorly maintained gravel roads to reach the distant hotels, there was often little they could do when they got there. They usually just joined the guests outside on the lawns watching the structure burn, hoping everyone had escaped. Occasionally, they managed to run in and save a few pieces of furniture and bric-a-brac that they kept for themselves if no one was looking. Or, if there were witnesses, they carried their acquisitions outside and set them down out of harm's way where everyone could see them. If the fire was in the village, however, the bucket-brigade sometimes saved a building and that was good for everyone's morale.

"It must be quite a fire," James said. "I've never heard the fire bells of all three churches ringing at the same time."

He got out of bed and went out onto the second-floor balcony of his substantial red brick home, from where, to his horror, he saw flames in the sky above the business section. Pulling on his pants and shirt, he shouted to his wife to stay home where she wouldn't get hurt. He then thrust his bare feet into his shoes, ran down the stairs, out the front door, and all the way to the blaze, a half-mile away. Only two or three members of the bucket brigade and his son Clem were on the scene when he arrived out of breath and fearing the worst. To his dismay, flames were already shooting out of the roof of his general store and smoke was pouring out of the windows of his guest house next door. The situation looked hopeless.

How could this be? James asked himself. *How can a fire, even in a wooden building, spread so fast?*

Other volunteers arrived, including two dozen men from the Indian Camp, and they formed a line from the river to the store, passing buckets of water hand to hand to throw on the fire. Without warning, a tremendous explosion blew debris onto the street and scattered the firemen.

"The fire's got to the gasoline barrels," Clem told his father. "There's nothing we can do for the store now. We'll try to save the other buildings."

James sat down on the ground across the street and let his son and the members of the bucket-brigade do what they could. Everything was beyond his control and comprehension. Were the fresh fruit and vegetables, tools, nails, spikes, cloth and clothing, coal oil and naphtha, cans of paint, turpentine and varnish, canned goods, barrels of cookies, boxes of raisins, jars of pickles and mustard, sacks of oats and chicken feed, sides of beef and pork, hundred-pound bags of flour and sugar, cases of dynamite and nitroglycerine caps, racks of hunting rifles, boxes of ammunition, axes, hoes, shovels and pickaxes, twine and baling wire, tubs of ice cream and cases of pop, and shelves of comic books and magazines all to be destroyed? What would his customers do? What would the tenants of his other buildings along the business section do? Was his insurance enough to cover his losses? Was he now a ruined man?

2

In the late 1850s, James's father, Reg McCrum, an Ulsterman and supporter of the Orange Lodge in County Armagh, Ireland, had read advertisements placed in the newspapers by the Canadian government. The District of Muskoka, a place no one in his small village had heard of, had just been opened for settlement, and it was first-come, first-served if you wanted free land. Single men were eligible to receive one-hundred-acre allocations and married men two hundred acres. All you had to do was to clear fifteen acres of the deep and rich land and build a sixteen by twenty foot house during the five years following the date of location and start planting your wheat and oats. Reg quickly married his long-time sweetheart, Wilma Brown, the daughter of a farmer on a neigh-bouring farm, sold off all his possessions, and left with his bride to become a pioneer in the new world.

But on arrival, they found Indians living on the land promised to them that they had to get rid of. Instead of flatlands ready for ploughing, his father and others like him from the Old Country got scrub hemlock and cedar bush right down to the water's edge. And after fighting their way through a jungle of underbrush to the white pine, oak, and maple farther back where the good soil was supposed to be, they found that the ground in most places all too often was only acid leaf mould over granite rock.

Before they could plant their crops, they had to cut away the small growth, chop down the big trees, roll the logs up into big heaps, and burn them in the spring. The summers were always too short, the black flies and mosquitoes unbearable, and the snow came early and stayed late. In those early days, they lived in lean-to shelters with mud floors and hemlock branches for roofs. There were no roads, no doctors, and the nearest grist mill was twenty miles away. But despite all the adversity, his parents and the other settlers who had arrived from the Old Country perse-vered. For had not the preacher who made periodic visits to their small community told them that God had sent them to the New World to build a New Jerusalem? Had the preacher not said that it was the destiny of the settlers to replace the Indians who were in the process of disappearing anyway?

His father had gone on to become the owner of the gen-eral store, the guest house, and the boat works, landlord of all the other buildings occupied by the other entrepreneurs in the business section, and the most generous contributor to the Presbyterian Church. What would he have said were he still alive and saw everything he had worked so hard for go up in flames? Thank God he had been carried away with his wife in the great Spanish influenza epidemic in 1917.

3

A fusillade of rifle and shotgun fire broke out as the ammunition in the general store began to explode, and the volunteer firemen, led by the war veterans who thought for an instant that they were back in the trenches, threw themselves to the ground. When the firing subsided, they rose to their feet just as cans of burning paint shot hundreds of feet into the air to land like flaming mortar rounds on the freight shed, on the boat works, on the shore of the Indian River. And as they rushed to put out these fires, the boat works burst into flames.

Someone yelled that Lily Horton, a university student from Toronto, working as a maid for the summer at the guest house, was trapped in her room. But no one moved, afraid of the flames and certain that Lily was already lost. That was when Jacob took action. He didn't think about what he was doing. Someone he worked with every day was in trouble and he had to save her. It wasn't any different from what he had done for fellow soldiers in danger during the battles in northern France. He went into the smoke-filled doorway, dropped to his knees, and moved up the stairs, keeping close to the floor where the air was clearer until he reached Lily's room. He pushed open the door and was met by a blast of heat that singed his eyebrows and scorched his face. But he pressed on, crawling on his hands and knees until he reached the girl lying unconscious by the window where she had gone to call for help. He took hold of her by the arms, pulled her out of the door, down the stairs, and out onto the street. Clem ran across and helped him drag her to the other side. The girl was dead and Jacob was so badly burned that he died within the hour.

4

Oscar had emerged from the water downstream from the business section and sat weeping on the shore as the fire bells continued to peal and the flames from the burning buildings shot higher and higher into the sky. In due course, unable to contain his curiosity, he went, still crying and with water dripping from his clothes, to stand as close as he could to the fire without attracting attention. He saw James McCrum rush up and anxiously confer with his son. He saw the men from the Indian Camp arrive and join the volunteer firefighters from the village in their futile battle with the flames. He saw his grandfather enter the guest house and emerge dragging the inert form of a teenage girl. He saw Clem go to help him. He saw his mother go to Jacob, kneel down and say something to him. He saw her get up and look around, obviously searching for him. He saw the angry look on her face as she came up to him and hissed, "It's all your fault. I hope you get caught," before hurrying away. He saw the men, with Clem in charge, carry Jacob away to the doctor's office.

Women and children from the Indian Camp joined him, not finding it strange on this night of surprises that he was soaking wet and distraught. An hour later, he heard the people around him say that Jacob had died a hero. In less than two hours, the entire business section was reduced to smoking ashes. Fire brigades from nearby towns arrived, but left shortly afterward, seeing that the fire had run its course and they were not needed. Tourists who had heard the exploding ammunition and gasoline barrels from their bedrooms and seen the great black smoke plume rising over the village from their cottage docks, arrived in their boats to inspect the damage.

James McCrum climbed up onto the back of a wagon and made an announcement.

"Today, our community has suffered greatly. The business section as we knew it is now gone forever, but I will rebuild it bigger and better, and everyone should be back in operation by next summer. Fortunately, we saved the *Amick* and I'm going to use it as a temporary store to serve my customers. Lily and Jacob we can't bring back. Both were the innocent victims of some arsonist's pleasure, for the fire would not have spread so fast if it had not been deliberately set. I feel so sorry for Jacob's grandson who is standing over there, grieving his grandfather's death. I promise that young man today, as God is my witness, that no matter how long it takes, I will find some way of paying him back for his loss!"

Too ashamed to face people who might come up to shake his hand and express their condolences, Oscar returned to the Indian Camp. Afraid of his mother, he hid in the bushes and watched the shack, trying to find the courage to go and try to explain why he had set the fire. She came out and went to the home of a neighbour who later returned with her to the shack. A half-hour later, the neighbour came out carrying the suitcases filled with the handicraft his mother had planned to sell to tourists over the summer. His mother reappeared carrying a packsack and started walking up the path toward the village. She had sold her handicraft to the neighbour and was leaving for the reserve.

Oscar left his hiding place and ran after her, determined to explain himself. Hearing someone behind her, his mother turned. "I want you out of the shack by Labour Day and I don't care where you go or what you do. And if you ever try to contact me back on the reserve, I'll tell the cops what you did and you'll go to jail for a long, long time!"

"But I did it for you," Oscar said.

"Did it for me! Burned down the entire business section and killed your grandfather for me! I never wanted you and knew from the moment you were born you'd be trouble, and I was right."

After her initial outburst, Stella said nothing further and walked away deeply troubled and blaming herself for her son's rampage. Her neglect had turned him into something as monstrous as she was. She wanted even less to do with him than before, because together they would destroy each other. As far as she was concerned, he was now on his own.

5

Oscar watched from a distance as his mother boarded the steamer that would take her to Muskoka Wharf Station to catch a train to the reserve.

Maybe she'll change her mind, he thought. *Maybe she'll change her mind and say she's forgiven me and ask me to come on board with her and leave Port Carling and all its problems behind.*

But the crew threw off the mooring ropes and pulled in the gangplank, there was a clanging of signal bells, a blast from the whistle, and the steamer left the wharf and headed downriver. Oscar waited throughout the afternoon, hoping desperately that it would turn around and come back for him. When it didn't, he walked slowly back to the shack and sat down on a stump outside the door. He now accepted that his mother had never, and would never love him, whatever he did to try to win her over. And through his own stupidity, he was responsible for the death of his grandfather, the only person, other than Old Mary, who had ever cared for him. He was now alone and didn't know what to do.

Friends and neighbours came out of the surrounding shacks and tried to console him.

"Jacob was a courageous man," some said. "Not many people would have gone into the building to try to rescue the girl. Your mother has gone off and left you, but that's nothing new. She's always been doing crazy things."

"Come home with us," others said. "Take your meals and live with us as long as you want. You shouldn't stay by yourself in Jacob's shack. You'll miss him too much."

Not believing himself to be worthy of such kindnesses, Oscar declined the offers, and the neighbours, thinking he needed time to grieve, left him alone.

Clem was the next to arrive.

"You poor little guy," he said, staring at him unblinkingly with his pale blue eyes and chewing a wad of tobacco. After spitting a stream of yellow juice into the bay and wiping his mouth with the back of his hand, he said, "You must really be feeling bad. Me and your granddad knew each other really good, you know, and not just here in the village, but overseas as well. We didn't always get along, but I respected him. He was a brave soldier, not chicken-shit like me. He was one of the best."

"Where's your mother?" he asked, "I need to see her."

"She's gone," Oscar said. "And I don't think she's coming back."

"That doesn't surprise me," Clem said. "Probably left you alone to look after yourself. Look, kid, I may be the village drunk, but if I can ever give you a hand, just come see me. You won't regret it."

6

Clem had first met Oscar's mother in the early summer of 1918 after being invalidated out of the army for shell shock — at least that was what the army medics had said, although he had another name for it. He had joined up in 1916, two years after war was declared, after convincing himself that his duty lay in fighting for King and Empire instead of staying at home and being husband to the wife he had married six months before. The army sent him in early 1917 as a member of a group of reinforcements to replace fallen and wounded soldiers in the trenches of northwestern France, where the men of the 48th Highlanders were located. As luck would have it, he ran into Jacob, who was a sergeant by that time, as well as a lot of the guys from the Indian Camp he'd known since he was a kid. Jacob was anxious to do what he could to help the son of his boss back home and asked his son-in-law, Amos Wolf, a smart, tough soldier, to stick close to him during the big offensives. The two men were the same age and they got along okay despite Amos being Indian and Clem not having any use for Indians before the war. Amos told Clem about meeting and marrying Stella, and when he got word she was pregnant, he was really happy.

Then one day, Amos said he'd had a dream in which the spirit of one of his ancestors had come to tell him that he would soon be killed and he was to ask Clem to go see his wife when the war was over. The spirit didn't say why, but Amos thought it was important that she know how he had been killed and have someone to comfort her.

"Why me?" Clem asked. "Why not Jacob? He's her flesh and blood, and he's here with you."

"Listen, white man," Amos said. "I don't question messages I get in dreams. If the Creator wants you to do the job, that's up to him to decide."

So Clem said okay, not wanting Amos to get mad. A lot of the Indian guys had been turning to their old beliefs during the tough-going. Who was he to say they were wrong? He didn't believe in churches and things like that anyway. So he agreed, never thinking he'd have to do anything. Not long after that, the big battle for Hill 70 took place and Amos and Clem went over the top with the members of the regiment. They hadn't gone far when a big shell came down not too far away. When Clem came to, Amos was just sitting there all glassy-eyed. The others probably thought they had been killed and had gone ahead. Clem picked up his rifle and told Amos they'd better get a move on.

But Amos just sat there with a crazy grin on his face. Clem gave him a good shake and tried to pull him to his feet, but he couldn't budge him.

"Save yourself, Clem," Amos said. "I'm already dead, just like the spirit told me in my dream."

"What's wrong," Clem said. "Where are you hit?"

"I haven't been hit, but I'm still dead and I want you to go see my wife like you promised when you get back."

"That's stupid talk. Let's get a move on before you get really dead."

"I'm already really dead, Clem. I'm really dead."

And since he was getting nowhere speaking rationally, Clem tried another approach. "If you're dead, then you can't be killed again. Grab your rifle and let's go."

And that worked. Amos got up all fired up to keep moving only to fall down dead. Really dead this time, from what, Clem didn't know. Bullet? Piece of shrapnel? What difference did it make? He was dead and he wasn't coming back. That's when Clem decided the war was over for him; he crawled into a big shell crater to wait out the fighting. When things quietened down, he joined up with what was left of the regiment and told Jacob he had decided not to kill any more Germans and had hid out during the fighting. Jacob never had any use for him after that, but told him just the same to pretend to be suffering from shell shock and they'd send him home.

"If you don't do what I say," Jacob told him, "they'll shoot you at dawn as a coward and I'll have to tell your father what you did."

❖

And so Clem went looking for Stella down at the Indian Camp in early July in that summer of 1918. He found her looking out the open window of Jacob's shack, went in, and told her that her husband had asked him to come see her if he was killed.

"So what's his message?" Stella asked after giving him a beer.

"He didn't give me no message in particular," Clem told her. "We chummed around a bit and he talked a lot about his son, and I was with him when he was killed."

"You came all the way down here just to tell me that!" Stella said.

"Don't you want to know what happened?"

"No, I don't. He's dead and I don't give a damn."

"Are you sure?"

"Are you deaf or something? If you can't take no for an answer, give me back my beer and take off."

❖

When Clem went home the next morning, he noticed for the first time the frilly lace curtains his wife had hung on the windows when he was fighting in France. He walked out, never to return. He realized that he had joined the army, not because his cousins and the other guys in Port Carling had already signed up, not because the Germans were bad and the British good, not because the Orange Lodge had said the Old Country and the Old Flag needed him, and not because his grandfather and father had told him to do his duty. He had enlisted to get away from his wife.

He had married her because she was pretty and liked to have fun and his cousins were getting married and his grandfather had told him it was time to do the same thing. But his new wife, who had agreed with his every action and utterance before their marriage, and who had thanked his parents profusely for buying and furnishing for them a small frame house with a good-sized veranda as a wedding gift, began to complain: "You drink too much. You don't go to church. You don't wipe your feet before you come in. You don't take baths. You stay out late at night drinking. You stink up the house with your pipe. You fart. Your breath smells bad. You burp. You spit your wads of dirty, foul chewing tobacco anywhere. You don't give me enough money to run the house. You won't ask your father for a high-paying job in one of your family's businesses. You won't help out around the house. You won't go to church ..." and an unending stream of the same.

After a wild night with Stella, however, Clem was determined not to spend his life with someone he had never loved and who nagged him. He wanted to live with someone who preferred acting to thinking, who believed only in her animal nature and not in God or man, who drank until drunk and then woke up and drank some more, who knew more swear words than he did, who would rather make love than eat, who didn't give a damn about what people thought of her, and who would certainly never think of putting curtains of any kind on the windows of his house.

His grandfather had left him some money and land within the village limits with a sparsely furnished dilapidated old house that had started life as a one-room log cabin built by a settler fifty years earlier. In the ensuing years, the pioneer had kept a cow or two, a few chickens, and a team of horses, and had scratched out a bare living as a teamster hauling logs out of the bush for lumber companies. When hard times came, he sold his holdings to Reg McCrum for next to nothing. Clem shared the money he had inherited with his wife and moved into the old house. As a favour to his father, who said that with most of the men still overseas, he had no one else to do the job, he became the master and storekeeper of the *Amick* on a temporary basis.

He told Stella he wanted her to come live with him at his new home.

"Bring the kid. I'll be good to him."

But she rejected his proposition, saying he wasn't man enough for her, although she was always glad to see him when he called on her at the shack during the 1920s. And if he didn't come to see her whenever she was at the Indian Camp, she would track him down and they would drink and fight together.

7

After Clem left, Oscar began to doze and soon lay down on the ground and drifted off into a dreamless sleep. He awoke the next morning before dawn to the strong smell of smoke and ashes in the humid night air, and with the conviction that his grandfather was inside the shack with a message for him. Jacob, he was well aware, was dead, but fatigue clouded his thinking, and so he got up, pushed open the door, and entered the building. But instead of his grandfather, something evil and repulsive lurking in the dark greeted him. He stumbled out, too shocked to be frightened, and went to the shore and sat down, his head in his hands.

He saw himself filling the can with coal oil, carrying it up the path in the dark, sneaking up to the *Amick*, spying on Clem, smashing the window of the general store, setting the building on fire, and running home in a panic after committing his dirty deed. He heard over and over again the clanging of the fire bells. He saw repeatedly the men battling the blaze, and worst of all, Jacob being dragged out by Clem and dying after his fruitless efforts to save Lily. Again and again, the events played out in his mind until he fell asleep from exhaustion and started to dream. Jacob was standing beside him on the shore and they were both looking out across the bay at the *Amick*.

"I'm sorry, Jacob," he told his grandfather, "I didn't mean to hurt anyone. I just wanted my mother to love me. You know what a wild imagination I have. I didn't know what I was doing until it was too late."

But Jacob, the grandfather who in life had never said an unkind word to him, had become angry and harsh in death.

"It was my shadow cursing you when you entered the shack tonight," he said. "I am dead but my soul is not on its way to the Spirit World over the Milky Way. The Spirit World does not and never has existed despite what Old Mary told you. And there is no Christian heaven or hell despite what the preachers say. After death, our souls go to a no man's land where they wander, bitterly conscious of their earthy transgressions, in an emptiness until the end of time. When you die, my grandson, you can look forward to sharing that place with me and Lily. And all of this death and destruction could have been avoided if you only had followed my advice and tried to fit in."

"Why did you do such terrible things?" Jacob then asked, his eyes as dead as those of the Manido of the Lake. "Why, why, why," he lamented, reaching down and shaking Oscar by the shoulder. "Why didn't you try to fit in?"

Oscar awoke with someone shaking him and saying, "Why, why are you sleeping out here in the open?"

It was Reverend Lloyd Huxley of the Port Carling Presbyterian church.

"I'm sorry to disturb you, Oscar, after everything you've been through," he said, "but I came down here hoping to speak to your mother, but nobody answered the door and I saw you asleep out here on the water's edge."

"My mother's gone. Gone for good," said Oscar, getting to his feet.

"Then who's looking after you?"

"I don't need anybody to look after me. I'm thirteen."

"But you're still a minor. Don't you have a relative who could take you in?"

Oscar shrugged his shoulders and Reverend Huxley changed the subject.

"The mayor asked me to look into funeral arrangements for your grandfather. Lily's family is going to take their daughter's body back to Toronto and bury her there. Do you think your mother would want your grandfather buried back on the reserve? Do you think she'd let the village honour him with a funeral service and burial here in Port Carling?"

"You'd have to ask her yourself, but she's gone back to the house on the reserve and there's no telephone there. Maybe the Indian agent could put you in touch. He's got an office on the reserve."

"I'll look up his number. In the meantime, why don't you move into your cabin or go live with one of your neighbours?"

When Oscar did not reply, the minister tried again.

"Then come home and stay with my wife and me until after the funeral. We've got plenty of room and you would be most welcome."

PART 2

1930 TO 1935

Chapter 4

DARK NIGHTS OF THE SOUL

1

Reverend Lloyd Huxley was born in China in the last decade of the nineteenth century and spent his early years as the only child of missionary parents among wars, rebellions, famines, and human misery in Sichuan Province. When he was a boy, his father told him that death and suffering were God's will and not to be questioned, and he had believed him. His father told him that it was God's will that he become a Presbyterian clergyman when he reached adulthood, and he accepted his judgement. His father told him that it was God's will that he become a missionary after becoming a clergyman and follow in his footsteps in China, and this he also promised to do.

But on his way back to Canada on the eve of the Great War to study theology at Knox College at the University of Toronto, Lloyd visited India, Mesopotamia, the Holy Land, Athens, Rome, Berlin, and London and developed a passion for foreign travel and international relations. He wanted to become a diplomat and make the world a better place and not a clergyman or missionary for which he had no calling. He wrote his father to ask his blessing to change his vocation, but the war intervened and he joined the army. During the fighting, he proved to be a skilled sniper, killing so many enemy soldiers that he lost count. At the end of the war, Lloyd returned to Toronto a decorated hero to find a letter from his father waiting for him.

"I believe in my innermost being that God wants you to bring the gospel to the heathen," he wrote. "Please make your old father happy and become a clergyman and missionary."

Lloyd did what he was told and enrolled in Knox College to train to be a minister, but he was plagued by flashbacks of the terrible things he had done in the war, and each night when he went to sleep he dreamed that something impure had taken root in his soul and he loathed himself.

How could someone so tainted with sin become a man of God? he asked himself. *How can I find redemption?*

He turned to prayer and asked God to forgive him, but felt no better. He looked for answers in the Bible, but had found none. Vague feelings of guilt, worthlessness, and a deep sense that life was cheap and had no purpose overwhelmed him. He went to see one of his professors, who had also been a soldier, and asked for his advice.

"Read the war poems of Wilfred Owen," the professor said, "and come back and see me. Like the laments in the Book of Job, they contain insights into the workings of Divine Providence. They helped me; maybe they can help you."

"Dulce et Decorum est" made the greatest impression on Lloyd, but he failed to see in it the workings of Divine Providence. It reminded him of the horrors he had just endured and provided him no way out.

Bent Double, like old beggars under sacks,
Knock-kneed, coughing like hags, we cursed through sludge,
Till on the haunting flares we turned our backs,
And towards our distant rest began to trudge.
Men marched asleep. Many had lost their boots,
But limped on, blood-shod. All went lame, all blind;
Drunk with fatigue; deaf even to the hoots
Of tired, outstripped Five-Nines that dropped behind.
Gas! Gas! Quick, boys! — An ecstasy of fumbling,
Fitting the clumsy helmets just in time;
But someone still was yelling out and stumbling,
And flound'ring like a man in fire or lime.
Dim, through the misty panes and thick green light,
As under a green sea, I saw him drowning.
In all my dreams, before my helpless sight,
He plunges at me, guttering, choking, drowning.
If in some smothering dreams you too could pace
Behind the wagon that we flung him in,
And watch the white eyes writhing in his face,
His hanging face, like a devil's sick of sin;
If you could hear, at every jolt, the blood
Come gargling from the froth-corrupted lungs,
Obscene as cancer, bitter as the cud
Of vile, incurable sores on innocent tongues, —
My friend, you would not tell with such high zest
To children ardent for some desperate glory,
The old Lie: Dulce et Decorum est
Pro patria mori.

The war poems, Lloyd felt, were the poems of the victims and the innocent and he was neither. He had enthusiastically supported the war, had enlisted as soon as he could, had volunteered to become a sniper, and during his time in the trenches had crawled innumerable times across no man's land to blow out the brains of dozens, if not hundreds, of German soldiers, men who usually had no inkling that the meals they were eating, the clothes they were washing, or the cigarettes they were smoking would be their last.

"You're having a breakdown. It's delayed shell shock," the professor told him when he reported back. "You have to remember that you aren't the only one around here who did appalling things in that war. We all did. We had no choice. Now grow up and get over it. You have God's work to do."

And as he had always done when faced with critical choices at other times of his life, Lloyd obeyed the voice of authority and continued with his theological studies. But the monster within his soul gave him no rest, and in time he began doubting the existence of the God of his boyhood and youth who now refused to answer his prayers. He nevertheless completed his studies in June 1923 and prepared to leave for China to join his father at the mission station. At the last minute, however, a member of the faculty approached him to say that the minister in Port Carling had retired. The process of finding a replacement would take some months and someone was needed to fill in on a temporary basis to serve the regular congregation and the tourists who attended church during the summer months. Could the newly minted Reverend Huxley help out on a temporary basis?

2

Reverend Huxley interpreted the request as an order and immediately packed, put on his clerical collar, and left for Port Carling. James McCrum and the other church elders were waiting at the wharf when he arrived on a steamer late in the afternoon on the first Sunday of July carrying his battered suitcase. James insisted that he come home to meet his wife and eat a good home-cooked meal. It just so happened that Isabel McFadden, a cousin of James and a teacher at the elementary school, had been invited to the same dinner; Isabel, florid-faced, long-necked, flat-chested, skinny-legged, unmarried, opinionated, and ten years older than the guest of honour, was a granddaughter of a pioneer and loved Port Carling to distraction. She had spent a year in Toronto at teacher's college after she graduated from high school and had been so homesick that she vowed that once back in Port Carling she would never leave again.

In honour of the distinguished guest, Leila brought out the family silver and porcelain dishes. Dinner was served in the dining room on a damask linen tablecloth spread over the solid top-of-the-line oak table James had inherited from his parents. They had ordered it, together with matching chairs and sideboard, from the Timothy Eaton mail order company in Toronto at the turn of the century. A large coloured print of "Good King Billy," iconic figure of the Orange Lodge, defeating the Catholics at the Battle of the Boyne in 1690, looked down on the dinner party from one wall. On another was a black-and-white tintype photograph of James's parents staring at the camera at a country fair in Gravenhurst in the early 1880s. Since it was a hot summer day, the door to the balcony looking down over the river was left open to catch the evening breeze.

Everyone bowed their heads and closed their eyes as James sought God's blessing for the food they were about to eat. Leila then got up to bring the platters in from the kitchen: roast beef, nicely overdone as everyone liked it, gravy, baked potatoes with sour cream, Yorkshire pudding, and carrots, peas, and salad from the garden. Afterward, as a special treat, there would be home-made vanilla ice cream with wild raspberries.

Isabel, who was seated beside Lloyd, tried to get up to help, but Leila told her there was no need.

"She's been helping me with the cooking all afternoon," she said, addressing herself to Lloyd. "She'll make someone an excellent wife someday."

During the meal itself, after Lloyd told her he had been raised in China, Isabel, with becoming earnestness, said that ever since she had been a little girl she had been fascinated by China and all things Chinese. "When my thoughts turn to China," she said," I think of Confucius and gunpowder."

"You have surprisingly good knowledge of China," Lloyd answered politely.

"Why, thank you, Reverend Huxley," Isabel said. "I've always been interested in other peoples and their cultures. When I was at teacher's college in Toronto, I even got to know a Chinese gentleman. He ran a small laundry close to my boarding house and I used to take my things to him for cleaning. Although he didn't speak English, he always smiled and bowed when I went in. I ate at a Chinese restaurant once, even though my friends told me I would probably be eating cat and dog disguised as chicken. I didn't like the foreign sauces but the rest of the food was quite good, especially the rice."

❖

By the end of the summer, without being too sure how it had happened, Lloyd was the new resident minister of the Port Carling Presbyterian Church. And although he didn't remember asking her, he found himself engaged to be married to Isabel, who had prepared her wedding trousseau many years before, hoping a man like him would come along. After she thoroughly inspected the manse, she concluded that all it needed to make it fit for her habitation were frilly white lace curtains on the windows.

When it took place the following summer, the wedding was a big affair. Reverend Huxley's parents came from China and stayed with their son at the manse. The entire congregation was invited and all the members of the extended McFadden and McCrum families came. Clem arrived at the church drunk and slept through the ceremony, but nobody minded. The wedding reception was held at the Orange Lodge and was catered for a modest fee by the Women's Orange Benevolent Association. Everyone had agreeable things to say afterward about the tea and coffee, the tasty egg salad and chicken sandwiches, the orange Jell-O with pieces of fresh fruit encased within, and the flaky crust of the apple and peach pies.

Life would have been good had Reverend Huxley not had ongoing nightmares about the war. In them, he saw himself climbing over the top of a trench in the middle of the night and carefully making his way to a secluded place in no man's land — a tower in a derelict church, a ruined house, a partially destroyed barn — anything with a view over the enemy's front line. At first light the next morning, he would begin looking for potential targets, almost always catching someone unawares, someone who thought he would not die that day. He would take one shot — never more than one to avoid giving away his position and drawing down hostile artillery fire — and another German soldier would be dead. For the rest of the day, he would lie concealed under a pile of mouldy hay, under a heap of rubble, under anything that would keep him from the enemy soldiers searching the area for the man who had killed their comrade. That same night, he would creep back to his own lines, call out the password, report to the sergeant, have something to eat, rest throughout the day, and go out after dark to kill again. And when that nightmare ended, it would repeat itself endlessly in his head until dawn.

As the years went by, and as he slept in his bed beside his innocent Isabel in peaceful Port Carling, his eyes in his dreams began to focus on the faces of the men he had killed. During the war he had shot the same man over and over again. The man might well have been smiling, crying, laughing, or scowling;

he might have had a fat face or a thin face; he might have been clean-shaven, bearded, or moustached. But he always shot the same man. And he always shot him in the same place, in the forehead. It had always been so easy, so simple to do. He would gently squeeze the trigger, the face in the scope would explode, like a pumpkin or maybe a squash when hit with a round from a Ross rifle. But as he relived those moments in the years after the war in Port Carling, his dreams unearthed details from his memory about each man that he never remembered recording, turning the universal target into individuals with hopes and fears and a wife just like Isabel.

Isabel would shake him awake when he moaned and tossed in his sleep and he would say, "It's just the war. The war makes me do that."

On the surface, Reverend Huxley was well-balanced and cheerful, a model husband who loved his wife, who was loved by her in return, a pastor who cared for his parishioners, and who was liked and respected by them in return. But on the inside, he was living an empty existence, pursuing a profession he had never wanted to follow, racked by guilt for crimes he had committed in the war, his soul taken by the devil, preaching a gospel he did not believe in to a people in a community where he did not want to live, and married to a woman he liked but did not love. All because he hadn't been able to say no to his father, to his professor, to James McCrum, or to Isabel.

But then, one day, during a trip to Toronto, he went into the Metropolitan Presbyterian Church in the downtown to wait out a rainstorm. He sat down in a pew and listened to the rehearsal of a massed choir, accompanied by an organ, singing Handel's *Messiah*, and when a soprano began to sing "I Know That My Redeemer Liveth," he felt a divine presence in the music. He turned to the poetry he had studied at the mission school in China and found spiritual meaning he had not understood before. Soon he was reading Shakespeare, Donne, Wordsworth, Newman, and Mansfield. T.S. Eliot's "Ash Wednesday" best reflected his new outlook.

> *Because I do not hope to turn again*
> *Because I do not hope*
> *Because I do not hope to turn*
> *Desiring this man's gift and that man's scope*
> *I no longer strive to strive towards such things*
> *(Why should the aged eagle stretch its wings?)*
> *Why should I mourn*
> *The vanished power of the usual reign?*

Music and literature had replaced the Bible as Reverend Huxley's sources of spiritual insight. God, in his own way, had answered his prayers, forgiven him, and given him peace of mind. And now, as he walked over the ridge back home after meeting Oscar, he felt elated. Perhaps there had been some divine purpose to the fire and to the deaths of Jacob and Lily. Perhaps it was to give him, Lloyd Huxley, the possibility of atoning for his war crimes by helping a luckless Indian teenager and giving him a chance in life.

3

The funeral service for Jacob, the most imposing held in the village since the ones for Reg and Wilma McCrum more than a decade before, took place at the Presbyterian church on the Tuesday following the fire. At ten fifteen, a church elder entered the vestibule, took hold of the longer of the two ropes hanging from the belfry, and, as he pulled it downward in long fluid movements, the bells began tolling slowly and mournfully the death knell for Jacob, giving notice to the public that the service would soon begin. At ten thirty, two dozen war veterans, twelve white and twelve Chippewa, all wearing their service medals, filed past the Union Jack flying at half-mast on the flagpole near the entrance, entered the church, and took their places. At ten thirty-five, the school principal and a procession of students and teachers marched up and formed a guard of honour on both sides of the walkway leading from the street to the church. At ten forty, the local members of the provincial and federal legislatures arrived in black limousines and were ushered in. At ten forty-five, the mayors and reeves of the surrounding municipalities took their places. At ten fifty, the mayor and councillors of Port Carling went in. At ten fifty-five, James McCrum and his wife, who were paying the funeral costs, entered and took their places at the front in the family pew.

The church was now almost filled to capacity, and the people from the Indian Camp and the villagers, together with a smattering of curious tourists, waited respectfully outside. At ten fifty-eight, a big black hearse arrived and a solemn funeral home employee wearing a black suit, black tie, and white shirt got out and opened the door at the back. Six pallbearers, three Chippewa and three white, all veterans of the Great War, stepped forward, seized the brass handles of the mahogany casket, and at ten fifty-nine, marching in step, carried it to the front of the church and placed it on a catafalque. Another solemn black-clad funeral home employee stepped forward, produced a Union Jack, carefully draped it over the coffin with his white-gloved hands, and placed on top of it Jacob's medals for valour in the war. At precisely eleven o'clock, Reverend Huxley, who had followed the coffin up the aisle, began the funeral service.

Oscar, who had entered with Reverend Huxley and Mrs. Huxley and taken the place assigned to him beside James and Mrs. McCrum, wept throughout the service. He was crying, everyone assumed, because he missed his grandfather, and that was partly true. But he was also weeping because the minister said Jacob had gone to a better place, and he now knew that was not the case. He was sobbing because Reverend Huxley said that God had seen fit to take Jacob home, and he knew that he, and not God, was responsible for his death. He was distraught because the Bible reading, chosen and read out by James McCrum, raging at the unknown arsonist like a fiery Old Testament patriarch chastising the Children of Israel, was *Vengeance is mine sayeth the Lord*. He was in utter misery because when he closed his eyes during the prayers, he heard only meaningless words. And when he tried to sing "Amazing Grace," the words left his mouth in a hollow whisper.

He was certain that God was punishing him for causing the deaths of Jacob and Lily and convinced that the appearance in his dream of a fierce, unforgiving Jacob was a message from the beyond, telling him he would go to hell after he died. Frightened, he prayed loudly and passionately, begging God for forgiveness for his sins. He had often heard the minister back on the reserve say in his sermons that the grace of God would wipe clean the slates of offenders and let them begin their lives anew. God always forgave sinners, the minister used to say, if they were sincerely sorry when they asked for it. Perhaps, however, he was not sufficiently sorry for setting the fire. He was certainly sorry for causing the deaths of Jacob and Lily. He was sorry for thinking ill of Clem. But try as he might, he wasn't sure that he was all that sorry for paying back the boys who pulled down his pants. Nor was he really sorry for punishing the villagers whose fathers and grandfathers stole the land of his people.

He glanced up at the stained glass window donated to the church by James McCrum in memory of his parents a decade before. In the past, whenever he attended church services in Port Carling, Oscar had found the engraving of a smiling Christ with a lamb in his arms knocking on a door in a garden comforting.

This time, however, the eyes of the Saviour were fixed on him and he looked mad. That was the confirmation of his worst fears. That was confirmation that his sins were so bad they were beyond divine forgiveness. He was destined for prison. He was destined to be shunned by all honest people. He was destined to wander after death in emptiness until the end of time, just as Jacob's shadow had said. Unable to contain his tears, he burst out into such loud and convulsive sobbing that Leila McCrum took him in her arms and hugged him. The choir began to sing and he joined in with such inconsolable fervour that Reverend Huxley and James McCrum exchanged glances and nodded their heads.

When the service was over and the medals and Union Jack removed from the lid of the coffin, the pallbearers once again took hold of the brass handles and, marching in unison, led the mourners outside to the hearse. Oscar whispered to Reverend Huxley that he wanted to go back to the Indian Camp. Reverend Huxley took him by the elbow and steered him to his car, whispering back to him that he had to go to the cemetery, that he had no choice. Opening the back door, he guided Oscar inside, then joined his wife in the front seat.

"You have to honour your grandfather," he told Oscar as he drove behind the hearse to the cemetery. "He was a hero in war and in peace. And if you aren't at the burial service, you'll regret it all your life."

It was only when they arrived at the cemetery that Oscar remembered that it had been built on land donated years ago by Reg McCrum from property taken from the people of Obagawanung. Jacob, he knew, with his need to be always accommodating, would not mind being buried among white people. But Oscar's heart told him it was wrong for his grandfather's final resting place to be among the pioneers who had expelled him from his place of birth. Bursting out once again into tears, he wrenched open the car door and ran to the Indian Camp only to realize when he got there that

Jacob's evil shadow now occupied the shack and he could never go home again. And with nowhere else to turn, he reluctantly went back to his room at the Huxleys'.

4

"I'm worried about him," Reverend Huxley said to James McCrum who had returned home with him after the funeral to discuss Oscar's future. "His mother didn't seem like a very responsible person when I spoke to her on the telephone the other day. She said that it didn't matter to her who buried her father as long as it wasn't her and that she definitely didn't want her son back. I must admit she sounded as if she had been drinking. The Indian agent, when I spoke to him, said his grandfather had already made plans to send him off to residential school until he was sixteen when he could look for a job. And although those schools apparently do a lot of good for Indian children, I'm not sure he would get the nurturing and attention he needs after the traumatic events of the past several days."

"My father always had a soft spot for Indians," said McCrum. "I must admit that I once had my doubts about them, but I changed my mind years ago. Maybe because I got to know his grandfather so well at the guest house and he got along so well with the other employees and the guests. He was a returned soldier just like Clem, but he became a sergeant and came out of the war in better shape. And I want you to know that I was serious when I told everyone the day of the fire that I want to help that young man in any way I can."

"It may just be an intuitive feeling," said Reverend Huxley, "but I think he could become a fine Presbyterian minister someday. He's the only child from down at the Indian Camp who has ever attended Sunday school and church here in Port Carling.

And you should have seen how passionate he was during today's service. I think he may have a vocation."

"I noticed that as well," said McCrum.

"I'd like to have him stay with me and my wife from now on and go to high school here in the village. I've already spoken to Mrs. Huxley. We don't have children and have plenty of room. If he does well, we could look into helping him study to become a missionary."

5

Mrs. Huxley couldn't understand why her husband had been in such a rush to take in the Indian boy. The day of the fire, he had gone to the Indian Camp to see about the funeral arrangements for old Jacob and that tourist girl, Lily Horton, and had come home to say he had invited Jacob's grandson to stay with them for a while, and he hoped she didn't mind. And after she reluctantly agreed to let him stay for a few days, Lloyd had said they should let him live with them until he finished his high-school education in five years' time. Maybe, he had added, they could adopt him, seeing as how his grandfather was dead and his mother, it seemed, didn't want him. It would be an ideal opportunity to help someone who was in deep trouble through no fault of his own.

Naturally enough, she had not been all that happy. Not that she had anything against Indians. After all, it would not do for a minister's wife, especially in a small place like Port Carling, where everybody talked and where everybody knew everyone else's business, to be prejudiced in any way, even if she believed Indians could never become fully civilized, however hard they tried, no more than tigers could change their spots. There was something wild, animal-like in their souls that set them apart from white people. You just had to look at them up close and see those black, unfathomable eyes. And Lloyd hadn't consulted her before inviting him to spend a few days in her home, although she was the one who would have to cook his meals, change his bedding, and wash his clothes. He probably hadn't ever seen a bathtub and wouldn't know about the need to make one's bed in the morning.

This Oscar boy apparently did well in the few months he spent at the village school each year. But he never smiled or said hello when she saw him coming from the Indian Camp in the mornings, and he didn't seem to have any friends among the other students. What did anyone know about him anyway? Maybe he was dangerous. Maybe he would steal the silver that had come to her from her grandmother who had brought it all the way from County Armagh, and run off and sell it somewhere if he took a dislike to them. She really didn't want someone like that around on a long-term basis. But Lloyd had said that ministers and their wives were expected to show Christian charity, if only to set an example for the other people in the community. He was so set on letting the boy stay with them, and seemed so happy with the idea of it, that she had agreed to let him stay until he finished his high school. But, she told Lloyd, the boy would have to help out around the house, bringing in the wood, taking care of the furnace, cutting the grass, putting on the storm windows in the fall and taking them off in the spring, and shovelling the snow in the winter. And others in the community would have to pitch in and do their share, especially James McCrum, who made such a fuss over him right after the fire.

And as for adopting him, she told Lloyd that she could never agree to adopt anyone that old. Maybe they could adopt an Indian baby, if he was so determined to have an Indian in the house. Baby Indians were cute and cuddly, but then all babies were cute and cuddly. And cute and cuddly Indian baby boys grew up to be great hulking, dark-skinned, black-eyed, black-haired, sullen, unpredictable teenagers, just like Oscar.

6

Oscar was worried when Mrs. Huxley knocked on his door and told him that Reverend Huxley and James McCrum wanted to see him in the study. *They know I set the fire,* he thought. *Why else would they want to see me? The constable's probably on his way to take me to jail.*

He entered the study and stood quietly by the door until Reverend Huxley saw him and pointed him to a chair. Oscar sat down, lowered his head, and stared at the floor like a guilty prisoner awaiting sentencing from a panel of hanging judges. No one spoke and he could hear the slow ticking of a grandfather clock from across the room and the buzzing of a fly, which he imagined had flown into the room by mistake and was now trying desperately to find a way out. He could hear the carefree shouts and laughter of boys playing softball in the schoolyard across the street drifting in through the open windows. It was obvious that they had not burned down the business section of the village and killed two people.

Why didn't they say something? He could take it! He could take the bad news!

He could stand the tension no longer. What was happening could not be real. He gasped for air as his tongue grew thick and he found himself floating high up in the room close to the ceiling. He looked down and saw James McCrum and Reverend Huxley hunched forward in their seats, earnestly talking to someone who looked exactly like him, someone who obviously was his double. They were saying things that made no sense: "difficult time … the Lord works in mysterious ways … destiny … much good will come from this."

Reverend Huxley, he then saw, turned to McCrum and said, "Stop, stop, it's too much for Oscar to absorb. Just look at his eyes. He's totally confused.

"Now Oscar," he said, "we are trying to tell you that the two of us want to be your benefactors and provide for your high-school and possibly for your university education. You have suffered a great loss and have no one to take care of you. Do you understand what I'm saying, Oscar?"

When Oscar's double did not respond, Reverend Huxley said to McCrum, "I'm sure he understands. He is an intelligent boy, but he's probably still in a state of shock from his grandfather's death.

"Now, Oscar," he repeated, "I want you to listen carefully. Mrs. Huxley and I have agreed to let you live with us for the next five years while you attend high school here in Port Carling. You would be expected to help out around the house like any other boy your age and get a summer job to help with the expenses."

"That's where I come in," said McCrum. "You can start Dominion Day working for Clem on the *Amick*. If all goes well, I'll give you a job at the general store when it's open for business next summer. And if your marks are good enough, when the time comes, I'll pay your tuition and living expenses at university. We should never forget," he added, "that the Lord works in mysterious ways. He caused that fire that took the lives of your grandfather and Lily Horton and drove away your mother for a purpose. And that purpose was to deliver you into our hands so we could help you fulfill your destiny. And your destiny is to become a missionary and take the word of the Lord to the Indians up north!"

"Do you understand what we are telling you, Oscar?" asked Reverend Huxley. "Have we made ourselves clear? Do you understand?"

Oscar at first did not understand. No one had mentioned the constable or jail. And was he really being rewarded for destroying the business section of Port Carling and causing the deaths of Jacob and Lily? That seemed to be the case.

"Thank you. I would like to be a missionary. I'm ever so grateful, ever so grateful," he heard himself saying. He then drifted down to become one with his double and to shake the hands of his benefactors who came crowding around speaking at the same time, saying "you are credit to your people ... take a few days off before starting work ... tired, you look tired ... go upstairs and get some rest ... yes, go upstairs and get some rest."

"Thank you, I would like very much to be a missionary ... it's always been my secret dream ... I'm ever so glad ... I'm ever so grateful ... ever so grateful," he said, before excusing himself and going to his room.

7

That night, Oscar lay awake in an unfamiliar bed, in a strange bedroom just down the corridor from people he scarcely knew. Although relieved he had escaped the constable, flashbacks of the fire tormented him when he drifted off to sleep and he woke up sobbing. Desperate to ease his conscience and bring his suffering to an end, he decided to go back to the shack and seek the forgiveness of his grandfather's shadow. Although afraid of what he might encounter, he slipped out of bed and hiked over the ridge to the Indian Camp, taking up a position in the dark under the cover of the white pines a hundred yards from the shore. From where he stood, he could see the moonlight shimmering on the water, and on the other side of the bay the outline of the *Amick*, moored as before to the government wharf. Other than the gleam of coals from a campfire left to burn itself out on the shore by a family that had gathered around it the previous evening to cook fried pickerel and bannock for their dinner, there was no sign of life in the sleeping community.

A dog barked, and someone yelled "Be Quiet," and the dog whimpered and was silent. For a moment Oscar was transported back four nights and he was standing on the shore looking across the moonlit bay trying to decide what he should do to get back at Clem and all the people who had ever harmed him and his people. A whiff of smoke and wet ashes returned him to the task at hand, and he crept up to Jacob's shack and looked into the window. At first, an impenetrable blackness confronted him. But then he made out a vague form, darker than the surrounding gloom, stirring in the obscurity of the interior. To his horror, the foul and appalling thing that had threatened him the night of the fire came into view, assumed the fire-scarred anguished face of his grandfather, passed through the glass, and came after him.

Oscar turned, his mouth open, too paralyzed by fear to cry out for help, and fled through the Indian Camp, back up the trail over the ridge, past the school, and up to the manse. The fiend kept pace with him, moaning and crying out in pain and anger. He pushed open the front door in a panic, slammed it shut behind him, ran up to his room, knelt down, closed his eyes, and began to pray.

"I'm sorry, God, for starting the fire that killed Lily and Jacob. If you could only forgive me and give me peace of mind, I promise I will never do a terrible thing like that again. Besides, it wasn't really my fault. The boys who pulled my pants down should share the blame. So should Gloria Sunderland who laughed when she saw my dick. And how was I to know that Clem wasn't to blame for beating up my mother. And please, please tell me that the shadow of Jacob was wrong and that the heaven of the Christians is real, just like my Sunday school teacher used to say. And tell me Old Mary was right when she said the souls of my people travel over the Milky Way to spend eternity in the Spirit World. I am terribly afraid of being punished for setting the fire and killing Jacob and Lily. I don't want to go to Hell after death or wander forever through time in spiritual emptiness. So please, please send me a sign, any old sign will do, to indicate that you have heard my prayers and have forgiven me."

But as he prayed, he once again felt he was just mouthing words into the void and he felt as alone and forlorn as ever. However, he refused to give up, and he prayed and prayed all night long, pleading, begging, arguing, and bargaining with God. It was his dark night of the soul, but when the first light of dawn appeared in the eastern sky, instead of spiritual release, he felt as solitary and lost as he had been when he started praying. There was only one thing left he could do: follow the lead of the Indian people who had travelled and lived since the beginning of time on this part of Turtle Island, and seek the guidance of the Manido of the Lake.

❖

When the Huxleys came down for breakfast at seven o'clock, Oscar was waiting for them at the bottom of the stairs.

"I'm going fishing," he said. "I want to bring you a fish to help repay you for what you're doing for me."

The Huxleys raised no objections, but after Oscar left the manse, Mrs. Huxley told her husband she was concerned.

"How can someone who has just suffered such a grievous loss go down the river on a pleasure trip? Doesn't he have any feelings? Don't Indians mourn the death of their loved ones like decent white people?"

Reverend Huxley interrupted his wife to say she was worrying unnecessarily.

"Different people mourn in their different ways. He's gone off somewhere important to him to try to come to terms with his loss."

"I find that hard to believe. I know Indians, and they don't act like that. I think he might be running away because he did something wrong. Maybe we were in too much of a hurry in deciding to take him in and in encouraging James McCrum to support such ambitious plans for his future. And if he does come back, I'm sure it will only be to sponge off all of us. And what are we to do if that mother of his comes around? She has the reputation of being a wild woman and a drunk. There are limits to Christian charity."

❖

Friends and relatives crowded around Oscar when he went over the ridge to the Indian Camp to prepare himself for his visit to the Manido of the Lake. They were sorry about Jacob, they said, but it was comforting to know he had died a hero and gone to a better place. Some people wanted to know why Oscar had slept outside the night of the fire, saying they had checked on him from time to time to be sure he was all right.

"You could have stayed with any of us," they said.

Others asked him how long he would be living at the manse. Someone asked if the Huxleys had a bathtub and if he had used it. What did the Huxleys eat for breakfast, lunch, and dinner? Someone else told him he was lucky to have been taken in by rich white people and asked him if he would be going to the Port Carling high school. "If you do," the questioner said, "you won't find it easy to get along with the white kids, but anything is better than being sent to a residential school. Your mother went to one of those schools and that's why she turned out the way she did."

Oscar didn't say much in reply. Reverend Huxley and his wife had asked him to live with them, he told them, and he had agreed. In the meantime, he was going to take Jacob's canoe and go down the river to do a little fishing and try to make sense of what was happening. But he didn't want to go inside the shack to get his grandfather's fishing gear. "Too many memories," he said. "Can someone go in and get it for me? And his pipe and a package of pipe tobacco as well?"

No one questioned Oscar's request. Although the people at Indian Camp were by now mostly Christian, they also believed in ghosts and witches, and they understood that Oscar was afraid

111

that the old shack was haunted. At first, no one would enter, but eventually an old woman, who, behind her back, people said was really a witch and able to cast spells on people she didn't like, went in and returned with the things Oscar wanted.

"Well, did you meet any ghosts?" someone asked her, joking.

"I did," she said gravely, but she didn't provide the details.

8

Oscar pushed off from the shore and began his journey downstream toward the mouth of the river. Smoke still rose from the ashes of the business section, but teams of workers were already at work clearing away the debris, the first steps to rebuilding. The *Amick*, it seemed, was doing a good business, judging by the number of shoppers on the wharf waiting to go in to make their purchases. All along the shore, summer residents were sunning themselves on their docks or going about their business in their motorboats. Crows and seagulls circled leisurely in the sky, on the lookout for the carcasses of fish and animals to eat. And when he emerged from the river and paddled out onto Lake Muskoka, Oscar saw children playing on the shore below the hidden grave of Jacob's grandfather. Life was returning to normal.

It was the first time Oscar had travelled on the lake since the trip he had made just two months before with Jacob from Muskoka Wharf Station to the Indian Camp, when a fierce cold wind had rattled the ropes of the flagpoles at the deserted summer homes on Millionaires' Row. At that time, the Manido of the Lake had been massive and forbidding in the cold light of early dawn. Now, in the bright sunlight and calm waters of the late June morning, it had turned into a sad, helpless old deity, no different than the rock from which it had arisen, out of place in the modern world ruled by the white man.

"Oh Great Manido," Oscar said doubtfully, throwing a pinch of tobacco onto the water and raising his arms in supplication as his grandfather used to do. "In trying to get even with the white man and gain the love of my mother, I brought about the deaths of Jacob and a white girl. Jacob's shadow then came to me in a dream, cursing me and telling me that after death there is neither heaven nor hell, nor a spirit world beyond the Milky Way. Send me a sign, Oh Great Manido, to let me know that it was mistaken."

The deity stared at him, sluggish and indifferent to his appeal. Oscar threw more tobacco into the lake and repeated his prayer, but the statue remained unmoved.

Maybe, Oscar thought, after waiting in vain for a response, *the Manido is really just a piece of rock and its powers come from people who want to believe it's a god. Maybe Jacob's shadow, which came in a dream with its message of hate and which chased me back to the manse after I went to it seeking forgiveness, is just a figment of my imagination. Maybe all Native devils, shadows, ghosts, and witches are just inventions people made up years ago to scare children. Maybe the Christian God, the Devil, and the saints are man-made imaginings.*

In a moment of epiphany, Oscar realized that if neither God nor the Creator nor all the panoply of lesser spirits existed, then he needn't fear spending eternity in Hell. He wouldn't have to pay for his earthly sins in the hereafter. He decided at that instant that Old Mary had been wrong, his Sunday school teachers had been wrong, the Presbyterian ministers on the reserve and in Port Carling had been wrong. There was no such thing as Divine Providence. There was no need for him to fear the wrath of God and Jacob's shadow.

"You don't exist, you never have. Now leave me alone!" he shouted out angrily at the sky. But as he did so, he understood he would never receive divine help to deal with the sorrow and guilt that plagued his waking and sleeping hours. But when he turned his canoe and began to paddle away, he heard the Manido of the

Lake laughing, and when he put his line in the water, he caught a fish.

❖

Later that afternoon, Oscar raised his four-pound pickerel up into the air and received the congratulations of the people who had come out to greet him.

"You take after your father," said an old man who had known his father before the war. "You're a lucky young man, since the family of a good fisherman never goes hungry."

"Did you make an offering to the Manido of the Lake?" someone else asked.

But rather than answer, Oscar walked up to the shack and went in. His bed and that of his grandfather were unmade, just as they had left them the night of the fire. His mother's ashtray, overflowing with cigarette ashes and butts, remained undisturbed and reeking of stale tobacco on the table. The supplies of tinned foods and packages of spaghetti, macaroni, and rice were in their place. Jacob's winter coat still hung from a nail on a stud, and his shirts, work pants, socks, and underwear were still neatly folded and stored on shelves in an open-faced orange crate. His wallet, where his grandfather kept his pay, which he always left beside the water pail, was missing, taken by his mother, Oscar assumed. Everything was in order and there was no monster in the shack.

A silent crowd was waiting when he emerged carrying a backpack filled with his clothes to take back to his room at the manse. Everyone wondered why he had refused to enter Jacob's shack in the morning but did not hesitate to do so in the afternoon. Something must have happened during his visit down the river that had made him change his mind.

Finally, someone asked, "Is Jacob's shadow still inside the shack?"

Oscar refused to answer.

Chapter 5

FITTING IN

1

When Oscar attended high school at Port Carling in the early 1930s, millions of men across Canada were out of work, people by the hundreds of thousands waited each day at soup kitchens to be fed, and municipalities were going into debt to provide relief payments to hungry families. Port Carling was not spared. Although the lifestyle of the people on Millionaires' Row did not change during these terrible years of the Great Depression, few people could afford to stay at the big luxury hotels and many of them were forced to close, their owners bankrupt. Teachers, accountants, and white-collar workers, who had no difficulty before the beginning of the hard economic times in finding the money to rent modest cottages for the season or to take rooms at reasonably priced guest houses, stayed away. The number of day trippers from Muskoka Wharf Station fell off to such an extent that the owners of the navigation company were forced to mothball half the fleet and to lay off their crews.

The boat works in the village closed its doors. Carpenters, electricians, and other tradesmen could not find work, and fathers found it hard to feed and clothe their families. James McCrum let it be known that he would provide credit at his store with no interest to hard-up families too ashamed to accept relief. Many people took him up on his offer. The village doctor began to accept eggs, chickens, sides of beef, and vegetables in lieu of money for his services. The older boys in high school began dropping out and leaving home, some to work for five dollars a month at government-run labour camps in the north building roads, but most hitchhiked to Gravenhurst and hopped freight trains heading West to join the army of unemployed in search of a job or a sandwich across Canada and the United States. The Chippewa at the Indian Camp and back home on the reserve, already living at subsistence levels, found it harder to get by. Fewer day trippers meant fewer sales of handicraft, but James McCrum, remembering the heroics of Jacob, treated them like the other villagers and let them run up bills at his store.

The Huxleys, as they had promised, provided for Oscar's keep. James McCrum ensured he was given one of the coveted summer jobs at his store, stocking shelves, bagging groceries, and, when needed, serving banana splits, sundaes, and cream soda floats in the ice cream parlour.

While still filled with shame and plagued by flashbacks of the fire, Oscar now devoted himself to fitting in as his grandfather had urged him to do when he was a little boy. In so doing so, he hoped he would be able to make amends with the white people he had wronged and appease the shadow, if such a thing existed, of his grandfather. If the white people wanted him to get an education, he would get an education. If the white people wanted him to become a missionary, he would become a missionary. If the white people wanted him to turn him into a brown-skinned white man, he would become a brown-skinned white man.

When Mrs. Huxley, with a pitiless look, told him he had to stop hanging out with his Indian friends if he intended to live under her roof, he cut off the ties with the kids he had grown up with from the reserve. When his classmates called him Chief, he pretended that that pleased him. When his grade nine teacher said that he should cut off his braid, "so as to not stand out," he pretended the idea was a good idea and he cut off his cherished braid. When he was in grade ten and won a district public speaking contest, he pretended to be happy when the well-meaning chairman of the school board at the award ceremony embarrassed him by telling the crowd that the Huxleys had saved him from a life on the streets by taking him in after his drunken mother had discarded him like an unwanted dog. When he was in grade eleven and had grown into a six-foot three-inch, two-hundred-and-thirty-pound, heavily muscled hockey player and the village crowd called him "Killer Injun" and told him to fight, he fought and pretended he liked beating in the heads of players from rival teams. And when Reverend Huxley arranged for him to enter Knox College in the fall of 1935 to study to become a missionary, he pretended that that was what he wanted to do.

Throughout the early thirties, Oscar was a familiar sight crossing the street each school day from the manse to stand in silence with the other high-school boys waiting for the bell announcing the beginning of the school day to ring. Sometimes, older students who had dropped out of school and gone off looking for work but had come home to visit their girlfriends and families for a few days before heading out again, would come by to gossip with their old buddies.

"You meet the damndest people out there riding the rails," they would say, reluctantly admitting Oscar into the circle of their intimates. "Some are professional bums who wouldn't take a job if it was offered to them. A lot of them say they're from farm families out in the prairies who lost everything in the dust storms to get pity and handouts. Some are perverts on the prowl who take advantage of the kids in the boxcars. Most are just like the guys from around here, looking for work wherever they can get it, as long as it's honest. All you gotta do to get started is get a bed-roll and grub sack and hop a freight. Every so often you jump off and go door-to-door bumming sandwiches in exchange for yard work. Sometimes they'll offer you some flour and eggs to make hotcakes. Sometimes, there's work available for a few months in a logging camp or on a farm during harvest time. The pay is lousy, but the food is usually good. Eventually you'll make your way to the border. That's where you better be sure you're well hidden in a boxcar when you cross over, since the railway cops are always on the lookout. Then once you're on the other side, you gotta pretend you're an American, for the folks down there don't like foreigners taking advantage of their goodwill.

"Best place to go is California," they would say. "Even though the place is overrun with starving Okies and Mexicans, you can usually find work picking cherries, apples, any sort of fruit and vegetables in season. It's all piecework, and if you're a good worker you can save a few dollars."

They would then talk about the good times on the road. About kind-hearted small-town cops who let them sleep over-night in the cells and gave them big breakfasts in the morning as long as they cleared out and didn't come back. About lonely wives who they claimed invited them in for a little lovemaking when their husbands were away at work. And about drinking cheap wine in hobo jungles and having the time of their lives.

But they had left home as boys and had returned as men with hard eyes as if they had seen things they didn't want to talk about, or done things for which they were ashamed. While they pretended they could hardly wait to go back on the road, you could tell they just wanted to stay home and get married and settle down like their fathers had done when they were their age back when times were good.

Oscar would then join the others slouching up the steps to the high school as if they were proceeding to their executions rather than to the singing of "God Save the King" and the start of the school day. But Oscar's reluctance was just an act. It was something designed to help him fit in and stay in the good graces of his classmates, many of whom were just putting in time until the Depression ended and the boys got jobs and the girls found husbands. In fact, Oscar loved school, and year after year was the outstanding student in his class. He was the only one who grasped abstract concepts easily, who had a feel for Latin and French, and who was able to talk intelligently to the English teacher about the books he was reading from the village library.

In time, his classmates began to treat him with wary respect; only Gloria Sunderland, embarrassed because she had laughed when the big boys had pulled down his pants so many years before, never spoke to him. He found it harder to establish good relations with Mrs. Huxley, who had made it clear to him from the outset that she wasn't fond of Indians and had not been pleased when her husband brought him to live at the manse. He did everything he could to make her like him, handing over his wages to help run the household, cheerfully helping out around the house, escorting her to church on Sundays, sitting beside her in the family pew, getting down on his knees and praying passionately and insincerely at her side, and, with eyes uplifted, joining her in singing the great old hymns, especially "Shall We Gather at the River," which through some buried memory always brought tears to his eyes.

At first Mrs. Huxley remained immune to his efforts, but one day she heard a knock on the front door followed by the sound of a woman speaking to Oscar.

"I've come to tell you that it wasn't your fault, Oscar, and you shouldn't blame yourself for Jacob's death. I'm to blame. I should've been a better mother, but I was afraid of what might happen if we got too close."

It was Oscar's mother talking nonsense, and Mrs. Huxley moved quickly to deal with her.

"I'm so sorry, Mrs. Wolf," she said, stepping in front of Oscar and naturally being as polite as a minister's wife could be. "But you're not welcome here. Please go away and don't come back."

"But Oscar's my son," Stella said. "I need him and he needs me."

"I doubt that very much," Mrs. Huxley told her, noticing the white flecks of spit on her lower lip and her lopsided smile — sure signs, in her opinion, of alcoholism. "Oscar doesn't want anything to do with you. And you've been drinking and don't know what you're saying anyway. You abandoned him just after he lost his grandfather in that terrible fire and we are taking care of him now. He's a lovely boy who needs the type of care only we can give him, so please go away."

"Tell her she's wrong, Oscar," Stella said to Oscar who was standing behind Mrs. Huxley in the hallway. "Tell her she's wrong. I wasn't always a good mother to you when you were small, but you're my baby. Come home to Mama."

But Oscar, whose mother had been dead to him ever since she had turned her back on him and boarded the steamer the day of the fire, and who was embarrassed by her display of drunken tears, turned and went upstairs to his room.

"See," Mrs. Huxley told Stella. "He doesn't want you. He doesn't want to live the same awful life you lead. Now please leave before I call the constable."

That was when Stella became really rude.

"Call the constable if you want," she said, shouting and using a lot of bad words unfit to repeat. "Stealing my son, and you a minister's wife! You probably can't make a child of your own.

Call the constable if you want and I'll tell him what really happened the morning of the fire. You won't think Oscar's such a lovely boy then."

Mrs. Huxley decided that she had heard quite enough and closed the door without saying goodbye, even if it wasn't good-mannered to do so. There was no point in trying to argue with someone who had had too much to drink. "People like that are liable to say anything," she told Oscar when she went to comfort him in his room.

Afterward, Mrs. Huxley couldn't do enough for Oscar, for in rejecting his mother he had proved to her satisfaction that he had left behind his savage nature and was now almost as civilized as a white person. In the mornings, when he came downstairs for breakfast, she would be waiting in the kitchen with a cheery smile to serve him bacon and eggs, fried potatoes and tomatoes, toast and Seville marmalade, Port Carling–style oatmeal porridge mixed with salt and pepper and melting butter, and English tea steeped to perfection. Every Monday, she would lay out on his bed for the coming week freshly pressed pants, shirts, socks, and underwear. In the evenings, when everyone gathered around the radio in the living room to listen to *Amos and Andy* and *Jack Benny*, she would make popcorn or homemade fudge and pass the tray to him before handing it to Lloyd. She even felt more comfortable discussing questions of religion with him than with her husband.

To tell the truth, it was a relief to have someone other than her husband to talk to. Although Lloyd must have known that he had told the same boring stories dozens of times, he wouldn't stop talking about his trip back to Canada on the eve of the Great War, when he travelled through the Middle East and the capitals of Europe. Sometimes, especially after he received letters from friends from the old days who had gone on to become diplomats, he gave the impression he was sorry he had become a minister and didn't believe in what he preached.

From time to time, Mrs. Huxley woke up in the middle of the night to the sound of weeping followed by laughter coming from Oscar's bedroom. She asked Lloyd what he thought might be happening. He said Oscar was probably just having bad dreams, and that was to be expected, given what he had gone through.

Oscar thus had his life in order and was happy, at least most of the time, for every so often, whatever he was doing — answering a question in class, reading a book, or eating fudge with the Huxleys in the evenings — he would remember that he was living a lie, even if he was just trying to fit in as his grandfather had wanted.

2

In his final summer at Port Carling, after he had finished high school and before he was scheduled to leave to attend Knox College, Oscar became close friends with Claire Fitzgibbon, a tourist girl from Forest Hill, Toronto, and a recent graduate from an exclusive girls' private school. They had first seen each other when Oscar was a thirteen-year-old working during the summer on the *Amick* when it called at the Fitzgibbon's summer home on Millionaires' Row to deliver groceries and other household supplies. He was on the top deck and she was standing with her brother on the dock. He looked at her and she looked at him, and both then turned to other things. To Oscar, she was just another overweight white kid, with braces on her teeth, light brown hair, pale blue eyes, and freckles, no different than the dozens of others he had seen over the years walking down the path from Port Carling to the Indian Camp shopping for souvenirs. Claire's eyes remained on Oscar somewhat longer, for it was not often that she saw someone with such black hair and dark brown skin.

When Claire went by motorboat with her mother the following summer to stock up on supplies at the newly rebuilt general store in Port Carling, she saw and remembered Oscar. During the next two summers, whenever she went shopping, she could not keep her eyes off the tall, exotic-looking Indian teenager who was stocking shelves in the store. The following summer, she went up to Oscar, who didn't recall seeing her before, and said she wanted him, and no one else, to carry her groceries to her motorboat. The other students working at the store for the summer noticed and teased him.

"Looks like you got an admirer, Chief."

"She's too rich for your blood."

"Watch out for her old man. He'll set the constable on you."

"You lucky bastard. What have you got that I haven't?"

By the summer of the fifth year, Claire had lost her baby fat and was a tall, well-proportioned young woman with dreamy eyes and straight white teeth. She now insisted on doing the shopping by herself, and when she saw Oscar at the store at the beginning of July, she didn't ask him to carry her groceries to the motorboat, although he did so just the same. One day after work, she was waiting for him outside the store and walked with him back to the manse, where they sat on bamboo chairs inside the screened porch until Mrs. Huxley asked Claire to stay for dinner. Afterward, she and Oscar went back outside and sat on the porch swing listening to Chopin piano music on a windup gramophone and talking for hours about things that were important to them.

Oscar told Claire his favourite piece of writing was *The Metamorphosis* by Franz Kafka. It was the story of someone who wakes up one morning to find he has been turned into a giant beetle, and even though he tries hard, he can't get out of bed to go to work. In the end, the hero accepts his new condition but has trouble communicating with his family and stops talking to them altogether. Sometimes, Oscar said, he felt like that bug.

Claire told him she was reading everything she could put her hands on by John Steinbeck and listening to the songs of Woody Guthrie to get a better feel for what the people of the Dust Bowl were going through. She hadn't yet decided exactly how she would do it, but someday, somehow, she would help them and people like them around the world.

Oscar told her he had promised Reverend Huxley and James McCrum to study to become a missionary to the Indians in northern Ontario, even if he wasn't sure he had a calling. But if that didn't work out, he would find some other way to repay them and the other people of Port Carling for the help they had given him after the Great Fire of 1930.

In the weeks that followed, Claire often came home with Oscar after work and stayed for dinner. In their discussions outside later on, she told him her parents only seemed to like going to dinners and cocktail parties with their friends in Toronto and spending time with the same people on Millionaires' Row and at the Muskoka Yacht Club. They wasted their time talking about their holidays in Europe and horse racing in Canada and the United States when people were out of work and going hungry. They wanted her to study art appreciation and home economics at university and then quickly find someone to marry from among their set, but she wanted more out of life.

At first the Huxleys were flattered that the daughter of someone from such a prominent family would spend so much time at their home with Oscar. But Reverend Huxley began to worry.

"Do Claire's parents know she's seeing you?" he asked. "Claire comes from a different world."

Oscar said he didn't know, but that it didn't matter. "Claire doesn't care about things like race and social position."

"I just don't want you to be hurt," Reverend Huxley said.

❖

By the latter part of August, the two friends had become so close that Claire invited Oscar home to meet her parents, Dwight and Hilda.

"Sundays are when we hold open house," she told him. "Everybody knows they can just drop in; no formal invitation is needed. We eat, joke around, and have a good time. Some of my friends from school come right after their morning tennis games. Daddy and Mommy's friends are always there. I'd like them all to meet you."

Oscar was surprised and gratified. His efforts to fit in were being rewarded by an invitation to mix with the cream of Canadian and American society. Assuming Claire had told her parents he was an Indian and that her family and friends had nothing against Indians, he immediately accepted.

On Sunday morning, a member of the household staff held Claire's motorboat steady as she and Oscar stepped onto the dock.

"I think I've been here before," said Oscar, "but I don't remember when."

"I know," said Claire. "I was going into grade nine and you were working on the *Amick* when I first saw you."

They then walked side by side up a recently raked, stone-lined gravel pathway past beautifully tended gardens of delphiniums, daisies, daylilies, and hydrangeas to the twelve-foot-wide flagstone front steps that led to an immense wraparound veranda.

"I'd like you to meet Oscar Wolf," she said to her parents, who were sitting on white cane furniture sipping gin and tonics and chatting with friends from nearby summer homes. "He's a good friend of mine and I invited him to join us for brunch."

"Why, it's that young Indian from the grocery store. Claire is always surprising us," her mother said, gazing unsmilingly at a place just above Oscar's eyes and ignoring his outstretched hand.

"How's business at the store? How's old McCrum making out?" one of the guests blurted out. But Oscar, taken aback by the frostiness of Mrs. Fitzgibbon's greeting, ignored the question and the conversation ended.

"Time to eat," Claire said after an embarrassing pause, and she led Oscar to the living room where brunch was already being served. A massive granite fireplace dominated the room. The floors were polished maple. Hand-painted light fixtures hung down from fourteen-foot ceilings and a wide circular staircase with a landing and built-in window seat led up to the second floor. Prominently displayed on a panelled yellow birch wall was a large black-and-white photograph of Claire's parents with President Wilson of the United States taken when the American leader spent his holidays at a nearby summer home before the Great War. On another wall hung a photograph of equal size of Claire's father dressed in the uniform of Commodore of the Muskoka Yacht Club. Silver cups, awarded to Claire and her brother for winning canoe races at the club's annual regattas, stood in a line on the mantel.

A maid handed Oscar a glass of freshly squeezed orange juice, a plate of scrambled eggs and bacon, and a large folded starched linen napkin. Oscar tried to open the napkin with one hand after balancing the glass of orange juice on top of his plate with the other. However, his hands trembled and he spilled some juice on the floor. The older guests exchanged small smiles and chuckles among themselves when they thought Oscar was not looking. Claire's friends, who had come to the brunch from the Muskoka Yacht Club elegantly dressed in their crisp tennis whites and cotton V-neck sweaters with navy blue trim, stared with barely concealed disdain at Oscar's clean work pants and plaid shirt and avoided speaking to him. Later that afternoon, when Claire took Oscar back to Port Carling in her motorboat, she seemed upset, but didn't say why. But the next day, when she went shopping for groceries at the general store, her mother accompanied her, and when Oscar said hello, mother and daughter pretended they didn't know him.

That evening, Claire telephoned Oscar to say how bad she felt not having answered his greetings at the store. She had no choice, she said, because her family had threatened to disown her if she saw him again. But that didn't mean they still couldn't see each other when university started in the fall. Toronto was a big city and they could find out-of-the-way places to meet and no one would ever need to know.

Oscar let Claire speak until she finished and then hung up without replying.

No one from the village, Oscar thought, despite their ingrained suspicion of Indians and occasional racist remarks, would have treated him in such a shabby way. But to be invited and then rejected out of hand by presumably well-educated people, not because of some personal failing but because of his race, upset him. The personal snub from Claire hurt even more because she had been the first friend his own age that he had ever had. She was someone who had shared his love of poetry, novels, and ideas, and someone he had permitted to penetrate the protective reserve he maintained with the people around him. He could not understand how a person so sensitive, idealistic, poised, and self-confident could so readily have obeyed her parents' wishes. It was always possible, of course, that she had just been pretending to like him and was just having some fun at his expense. He hoped not, because he liked her, and although he had been too upset to speak to her when she called, he fully intended to find some way of getting together with her in Toronto in the fall as she had suggested.

The other employees of the store who had been present when the brush-off took place felt sorry for Oscar, even if they were not surprised at the outcome. After all, it wasn't the first time that outraged parents from Millionaires' Row had put a stop to a budding romance between a daughter and a local boy, although to best of anyone's recollection it was first time that the local boy had been an Indian. The story of the failed romance between the rich girl and the poor Indian was then repeated from employee to employee, becoming more and more distorted with each telling until a breathless sales clerk, anxious to curry favour, went into the office of James McCrum to give him all the salacious details.

"You just gotta hear this, Mr. McCrum," she said. "Everyone in the village is talking about Oscar and the Fitzgibbon girl. And I have it from a good source that they've been having a hot love affair all summer long without anyone knowing about it. They apparently got together out on the porch at the manse every night after the Huxleys went to bed and did things they shouldn't have. Poor Reverend Huxley and his wife didn't have a clue what was going on under their noses. Sometimes, they went out in her motorboat and anchored it and continued their carryings on. Finally, her parents caught them in the act in the boathouse at their place down on Millionaires' Row and told him to leave their daughter alone. And apparently there was a lot of drinking going on and someone said she was pregnant."

"What a bunch of hogwash," McCrum told her. "I don't believe a word of it, and if I were you, I wouldn't go around spreading rumours about a fine, outstanding boy like Oscar!"

But he immediately called Reverend Huxley to get his version of events.

"It was an innocent relationship between a young man and a young woman, and I'm sure nothing untoward happened," Reverend Huxley told him. "But Oscar did accept an invitation to brunch at Claire's place and her parents must have told her she couldn't see him again."

❖

"I'm sorry those people on Millionaires' Row treated you so badly," Reverend Huxley said to Oscar after inviting him into his study and asking him to sit down beside him on the sofa. "You don't have to talk about it if you don't want to. We all go through these crises in our lives. Sometimes we just need to put them in perspective."

"I'll know better the next time, if there is a next time," Oscar said, glancing at the door and waiting for the interview to end. "But there's no need to worry. No one got hurt."

Reverend Huxley rose and took a book from a shelf. "Books and literature can help people overcome bad times in their lives," he said. "It's a truism, but I speak from personal experience. This novel, for example, is by Erich Maria Remarque, a German veteran, and in my opinion the best book written on the Great War. It's called *All Quiet on the Western Front*. It allows us to see the war from the other side's perspective and to understand that we are all people, that we are all human. When you read books like this, you are not an Indian, you are not a white man, and you are not a Frenchman, German, Spaniard, or Italian, or rich or poor. You are a human being with the same hopes, the same fears, and the same dreams as everybody else. And when you finish this one, I want you to start on the others I've collected over the years. Maybe they'll change the way you look at things. Maybe they'll help you put the behaviour of people like the Fitzgibbons in perspective as you go through life. There are lots of people out there just like them."

Oscar took and read the book, but it didn't make him feel any better. And his problem wasn't just with the Fitzgibbons and people from their social set. After five years of living with the Huxleys, doing well in school, playing hard in sports, and doing everything his benefactors expected of him, he still didn't fit in. He was still the outsider. And now he was expected to leave for Toronto to study to be a missionary when he wasn't even sure he believed in God.

He needed to talk to someone he could trust, someone he could count on to tell him the truth, someone who could let him know whether he should carry on trying to fit in or whether he should drop the whole thing once and for all. That was when he decided to call on Clem McCrum, who had once told him to come see him if ever he could help and who had treated him well when he worked on the *Amick* the summer after the fire.

Chapter 6

THE RUPTURE

1

Tired of being polite to the wealthy tourists who shopped on the *Amick*, Clem quit his job in the spring of 1931, bought a dozen cows, and started up a small dairy operation on his farm. The sign on his laneway read as follows:

ROCKFACE DAIRY

RAW MILK FOR SALE

BRING YOUR OWN JUGS

Although the sale of unpasteurized milk was illegal, Clem was soon swamped with business from people who said his milk was frothier than pasteurized milk, from mothers who claimed it was full of vitamins to chefs at the big hotels around the lakes who maintained that it made their pastries, cakes, and mashed potatoes taste better. Inspectors from the District Health Board paid him a visit and were displeased to find chickens drifting in from the outside through the open door to the dairy, shitting on the floor, hopping up to grip the rims of the pails of milk with their dirty feet, plunging their heads up to their necks in the liquid, raising their beaks appreciatively and swallowing their fill.

Clem brushed aside the complaints. "When I was a kid growing up around here, we drank raw milk all the time and nobody got sick."

"But times have changed, Mr. McCrum," the inspectors said. "You must clean up your dairy and pasteurize your milk or we'll put you out of business."

To obey the letter but not the spirit of the law, Clem put up a new sign on the gate.

ROCKFACE DAIRY

RAW MILK FOR PET CONSUMPTION

BRING YOUR OWN JUGS

His business grew bigger. And as the years went by, he became more and more eccentric, refusing to shave, cut his hair, or take baths on the grounds that someone who sold raw, natural milk should himself be a raw, natural man. Occasionally, to establish a closer connection to nature in all its glory, he would walk naked through the village during violent summer storms and let the warm driving rain purify his body. He stopped washing his clothes and wore the same ragged pair of overalls held up by a single brace until they disintegrated and fell off his body. He gave up drinking whiskey, saying it was produced in factories and thus unnatural, and he made and drank his own homebrew out of dandelions and chokecherries. When Stella came to see him in the summers, they would drink too much and stagger downtown, shouting and quarrelling with each other and with anyone they met, making a public

JAMES BARTLEMAN

spectacle of themselves before curling up and sleeping off their drunks on the steps of the Presbyterian church.

In the end, however, the people in the village turned against him. In the past, when Clem got drunk and lurched his way through the village, everyone used to laugh and say "That's just good old Clem having a good time. He means no harm," and they would stop and joke and laugh with him. When they looked out their windows during thunderstorms and saw him walking naked, they laughed as well. When he fell asleep on the side of the road one winter during a heavy snowstorm after drinking too much and a snowplough buried him alive and he wasn't rescued until the next day, he became somewhat of a local hero. People would point at him and tell their friends, "That's the guy who had so much alcohol in his blood, he didn't freeze to death when he spent the night in a snowbank."

Now nobody laughed. "That man is a menace," tourists from Millionaires' Row told the leading citizens. "When we park our motorboats at the government wharf, he's always there drunk and making rude comments. When we tell him to grow up and leave us alone, he becomes angry and you never know if he's going to hit you. He doesn't even care if there are children present when he sings his dirty songs."

The constable took Clem aside and tried to reason with him. "You know, Clem, we go back a long way. You used to raise hell when you were a kid, but I thought those days were long over. I'd really be sorry if I had to arrest you. So for your own good, if you gotta get drunk, for God's sake do it at home and sleep it off in your own bed, otherwise I'll have to take you in. And put some clothes on if you gotta be out and about in the thunder and lightning. You're not a pretty sight."

But Clem just laughed, and he laughed harder when he was arrested and hauled up before the magistrate and fined ten dollars for public intoxication. The wife he had left years earlier resurfaced and told everyone that the day he had walked out on her was the happiest day in her life. She had always thought, she said, there was something wrong with his head, and his wandering around in his birthday suit just proved it. She spoke to her blood relatives, who were also Clem's blood relatives, and turned them against him. Clem's own father, infuriated at his son's public drunkenness and his general lack of decorum, and embarrassed that a member of his family would run after an unruly Indian widow, let it be known that after much prayer and reflection, he had cut him out of his will. Clem carried on as before.

Having noted that Clem's popularity in the community had fallen, and confident there would be no outcry if they took firm measures, the members of the Muskoka District Health Board found the courage to force him to shut down his dairy business, but he just branched out into hog farming. However, his pigs burrowed under the fences he put up around his pigpens and were always escaping and running through the village, grunting and squealing and uprooting vegetable gardens and frightening children and old women. The magistrate fined him five dollars for violating village ordinances, but after Clem handed over the money, he went home and defiantly opened the gate to the enclosure and let his swine roam the village as before.

"I got the money to pay the fines," he told anyone who would listen.

That was when the village council decided that enough was enough. It just so happened that the old village dump, which had served the needs of the community and surrounding summer resorts for the previous fifty years, was spilling over with garbage and swarming with rats and other vermin. A new one had been urgently needed for years, but each time officials proposed a new dumpsite, the people who lived in the vicinity came with their friends to meetings of the council to complain and no action was ever taken. Clem's isolation within the community, however, gave the council the opportunity it needed. It expropriated the necessary land from his holdings, built a garbage dump behind his house, and constructed a road that passed less than twenty feet from his front door to reach it.

As the council had foreseen, no one, not even Clem's father, protested its action. To ensure everyone knew where the new facility was located, municipal workers erected a ten-by-fifteen-foot sign at the entrance to the new road that helpfully pointed out that new dump was open twenty-four hours a day to accept "Household, Institutional and Construction Waste of all Kinds." Clem, they expected, would be so disgusted by the sights and sounds of garbage trucks passing by his house that he would give up and leave the village, never to return. That, at least, was the council's hope.

❖

Clem poured himself a tumblerful of dandelion wine and offered one to Oscar.

"Thanks, Clem, but I don't think your father and the Huxleys would want me to start drinking."

Clem listened to his story with a deepening frown.

"Goddamn it, Oscar," he then said. "Wake up to the fact you're alive! Its time you grew up and lived your own life. You're an Indian, for God's sake. You don't need anyone's permission to have a little drink. You don't belong with those snobs on Millionaires' Row, and for that matter you don't belong among the people of this village. The folks around here don't really trust you. They think you're a fake. They think there's something phoney about your attempts to be one of them, as if it was all an act."

"I don't think Reverend Huxley feels that way," Oscar said.

"As far as the Reverend and his friends go," Clem replied, "you probably could play along with their plans and be one of them someday. But if you do what they say and become a missionary, you'll spend the rest of your life going to church on Sundays, living in a house with white lace curtains, and spending your time with stuffed shirts who don't smoke or drink. I've known from the beginning you set that fire back in 1930 and have been trying to make amends ever since by sucking up to everyone."

"Maybe I'll have a drink of your wine after all," Oscar said, sitting up straight in his chair.

"I saw you peeking in the window of the *Amick* just before dawn early that June morning," Clem said, as he poured a glass of homebrew for Oscar. "The sun wasn't even up. One minute you were there, the next you were gone. Then all hell broke loose, the fire bells started to ring, and the old general store went up in flames. It had to be you. No one else was around at that time. You musta had your reasons, I thought, and you probably never figured it would spread like that."

"I didn't think anyone knew my secret," Oscar said, after quickly swallowing a half a glass of wine, the first alcohol he had ever tasted.

"Don't take me for a fool."

"I wouldn't do such a thing today."

"I hope not. I wouldn't let you off a second time."

"There are a few things about what happened afterward, Clem, that I've wondered about over the years."

"Like what?"

"Like why your father and Reverend Huxley have been so good to me."

"I haven't the slightest idea, Oscar."

"Do you think they've been helping me because I'm an Indian and they stole the land of my people? Because they feel guilty?"

"What do you mean stole the land? There are only a few old-timers around who remember there was an Indian village here when they came to take up their land grants."

"Then who's to blame?"

"Why, nobody's to blame. People in those days was just doing what they had to do to make a living. Nobody had any choice."

"Somebody's got to take responsibility."

"Okay, let's look at the matter a little more closely. The young people of today are not to blame because they weren't around in those days. The settlers aren't to blame because they just took the land the government gave them. The government in power at that time isn't to blame because it was following the policies of the governments before them, taking the lands from the Indians to give to settlers to develop. The British aren't to blame because they had turned over responsibility for the Indians to the Canadians when they pulled out. Christopher Columbus isn't to blame since the kings and queens over there in Europe sent him over here. So who can you blame? You can't blame nobody!"

"I still think your father and others are helping me to make amends for what the settlers did to my people," said Oscar.

"Well, I don't," said Clem, "and I know them better than you. And they'll drop you without a second thought if you ever step out of line. But now that I've given you some free advice, I'd like you to help me pay back the people around here who've shown *me* no respect."

"I once tried to get even, Clem, and it didn't turn out the way I wanted."

"But this is different, Oscar. I'm not planning to burn down the village."

"Whatever you say," Oscar said, his mind now deadened from the wine. "You can count on me."

"I got dynamite. Ever since everybody turned nasty, I've been quietly buying and storing lots of it. Things have come to a head and I want you to help me blow a hole in their goddamn road so big they'll never be able to fix it. That'll learn them not to mess with Clem McCrum.

"Did I ever tell you my story about the constable and the outhouse?" he asked, fetching a gallon jug of pickled eggs. "Help yourself," he said after unscrewing the lid. "You shouldn't drink dandelion wine without pickled eggs, and I made them myself."

"The constable and the outhouse? I don't think you ever did," Oscar said, biting into an egg and almost gagging on the taste of the strong vinegar.

"The constable was always chasing after us kids and giving us a hard time when all we were doing was having a little fun," Clem said, pouring both of them tumblers of wine. "And so one Halloween we decided to get him. We waited until after dark and snuck around to the back of his house and moved the old outhouse a few feet down the path, just enough to leave the hole full of crap unprotected. We lay in wait and held our breath, hoping just the constable and not his family would fall into our trap. Finally, the back door opened and out came the constable himself, puffing on his pipe, without a care in the world. And sure enough, just as he reached for the handle of the outhouse door, he fell into the hole. He was waist-deep in shit and not happy. You could've heard him yelling right down to the Indian Camp. His wife and kids came out and they got him madder by laughing. They couldn't stop laughing, and neither could we. But we took off right away since we didn't want to get caught. What made it worse for that poor guy was that the next day everybody in the village knew the story and kept rubbing it in. I think in the end he found out who the culprits were but he never came after us. He was too embarrassed."

Clem then told dozens of other tales from his boyhood and youth and Oscar responded with stories about life back on the reserve when he was a boy, and about things he had had to do to keep Mrs. Huxley happy over the past five years that in retrospect seemed funny. By now firm friends, they laughed and joked and drank all night, staying up to witness the dawn chorus of seagulls, crows, and vultures sitting on dead tree branches and circling high over the burning garbage at the dump. They carried on carousing until mid-morning when the church bells began to echo throughout the village announcing the imminent start of Sunday services.

"We gotta get this done when everyone is still in church," Clem said. "They'll all be scared shitless when they hear the blast."

They then made repeated trips to carry three dozen cases of dynamite from Clem's cellar and stuff them into the culvert at the T-junction where the dump road joined the highway through the village. Clem swiped a match on the seat of his pants, lit a fuse, and he and Oscar ran for cover. The ensuing explosion rained rocks and stones down on the village, shattered windows for miles around, sent cattle and sheep grazing on nearby farms fleeing in panic, led dogs to howl, disrupted services in all three churches as Clem had hoped, splintered the expensive stained glass window donated to the church by James McCrum, and was even heard by the guests assembling for Sunday brunch at the Fitzgibbons' summer home on Millionaires' Row.

"How odd," Hilda Fitzgibbon said to her husband. "It's thundering out and there isn't a cloud in the sky."

"I wouldn't worry about it, my dear," Dwight said, and he resumed providing his views to Claire on the studies she should follow when she registered at the University of Toronto during the week to come.

❖

Although two hundred yards up the road, Oscar and Clem were lifted off their feet by the blast and thrown to the ground. Both got up unhurt and laughing. "That'll show those bastards they can't tangle with me!" Clem yelled.

Deaf from the explosion, Oscar could only guess at what Clem was saying, but he didn't wait around to learn more. A stupendous cloud of dust was rising hundreds of feet into the air, obscuring a crater blasted out of the ground fifteen feet deep and twenty feet wide. All that remained of the trees for a good fifty yards into the bush were their trunks, sheared off ten feet above the ground. Oscar fought his way through the debris of broken branches around the hole and made it to the highway as the fire bells of all three churches began clanging, summoning the volunteer firemen to assemble at the fire hall.

Reverend Huxley, James and Mrs. McCrum, and the other parishioners of the Presbyterian church had evacuated the building and were outside looking up the street in the direction of the blast when Oscar came into view, his shirt-tails hanging out, covered in dust, his head down, and walking fast.

"Oscar, Oscar, what's going on?" James McCrum called out as he drew near.

"Were you hurt in the blast, Oscar?" Reverend Huxley shouted to him as he went by. "Was anyone hurt, Oscar? Stop, Oscar, come back and tell us. We need to know."

Oscar paid no attention. His ears were ringing, he was drunk, and he just wanted to find some place to lie down and sleep in peace.

2

The next morning, Oscar woke up shivering, covered in dew and lying on the ground in front of his grandfather's shack where he had hid out until he was sober enough to go back to the manse. His head was aching, the taste of sour homemade wine and pickled eggs polluted his mouth and breath, and he had a thirst no amount of river water could quench.

"Where were you?" Mrs. Huxley asked him when he walked unsteadily through the door of the manse. "Why didn't you come home last night? Didn't you know we would be worried? In case you hadn't noticed, we're responsible for you."

"I don't think we have time to get into all that, Isabel," Reverend Huxley said, interrupting his wife.

At the breakfast table that same morning, she had surprised him by the virulence of her remarks about Indians and Oscar.

"You can take these people out of their shacks and help them live like civilized white people," she had said. "But they revert to type sooner or later. I bet he's going to walk away from the chance of going to university despite everything we've done for him. And in these hard times it wasn't always easy."

While not as outraged at Oscar's behaviour as his wife, Reverend Huxley was deeply disappointed and told him so on the drive to the railway station.

"Everyone was looking forward to your attendance at church yesterday," he said. "I had a special sermon prepared to bid you farewell as you embarked on your new life. James McCrum was going to speak. The choir was going to sing "Shall We Gather at the River." That was all ruined. Why didn't you come afterward and tell me what you had done and say you were sorry? Why didn't you come home last night? Maybe you were trying to pretend nothing had happened, but you didn't fool me. I was a soldier and I know a drunk when I see one."

As Oscar resisted the urge to vomit out the window, Reverend Huxley said that he had forgiven him. "And James McCrum, after much thought and prayer, has forgiven you as well. He is a true Christian who believes in the power of forgiveness and redemption and has faith that you will do great things with your life despite this setback."

In fact, Reverend Huxley had found it hard to calm McCrum down.

"Clem has once again disgraced the family name," McCrum had said. "And to think I once thought he would take over McCrum and Son! But he will pay the price for his vandalism with a spell in jail. Oscar, however, has thumbed his nose at us by behaving like any ordinary drunken Indian."

It had taken all of Reverend Huxley's powers of persuasion to persuade McCrum to honour his promise to fund his university education.

"I'm now inclined to think there was some truth to rumours that he and that Fitzgibbon girl were sneaking around drinking and up to no good all summer behind your back," he told Reverend Huxley. "But for his grandfather's sake, I'm prepared to give him one last chance."

❖

Oscar slept all the way on the train to Union Station in downtown Toronto and took a streetcar to the University of Toronto where he joined the lineup of students waiting to register for their first-year courses. An envelope containing a money order from James McCrum, made out to the university to cover his tuition and residence costs for the year, was in one pocket; in another pocket was the ten dollars Mrs. Huxley had let him keep for spending money after he had handed over the wages he had earned working at the general store over the summer. He looked around the room hoping to see a friendly face, ideally another Native student who wouldn't reject him if he were to walk up and extend his hand and say, "I'm Oscar Wolf and I'm new here. I guess you're new as well. Let's be friends."

But there were no brown faces in the room, or for that matter any black or yellow ones. Instead, a mass of anxious eighteen- and nineteen-year-old white high-school boys with a sprinkling of white women the same age milled around clutching their acceptance letters in their hands, looking for the right line to join to register. Those with sunburned faces and red necks, he guessed, were probably the sons and daughters of farmers. Others, with their pale complexions, he supposed might be the offspring of small businessmen, clergymen, doctors, lawyers, and teachers.

One group stood out from the others by the elegance of their clothing, by their perfect tans, and by their self-assurance. Claire, he saw, was one of them, and although she stared directly at him, she gave no hint she knew him.

I don't want to do this, Oscar thought, looking away. *I don't want to be subjected to constant brush-offs from Claire. I don't want to be humiliated again by the students who were at the Fitzgibbon's brunch. I don't want to spend the next three or four years of my life here with no friends and as the only Native student on campus. I don't want to spend the money of someone whose store I destroyed. I don't want to keep up the pretence that I have a religious calling when I'm not sure I believe in God. Clem told me I shouldn't try to be something I wasn't by trying to fit into the white man's world. It's time I was honest with myself. I've got to return to Port Carling and confess my crimes and betrayals to my benefactors and beg their forgiveness. And since they like me so much, they'll forgive me and I'll be free to leave and do whatever I want.*

But as he walked back to Union Station to take the train back to Muskoka, Oscar had second thoughts. Confessing everything and accepting the consequences of his misdeeds would certainly be the honourable thing to do, but what if Lily Horton's family was to learn of his confession? They would be forced to relive the grief they suffered when they first learned of their daughter's death. What if his benefactors were not to forgive him? What if the Hortons and his benefactors were to call the police? The police would charge him with arson, manslaughter, and murder, and he would be sent to jail for many years; he might even be sentenced to death and be hanged in the district jail.

Stretched out on a hard wooden bench in the waiting room in Union Station, with his coat as a rudimentary pillow and unable to sleep, Oscar spent the night reflecting on his options. By the time he bought a ticket for the first leg of the journey to Port Carling, he had persuaded himself that sparing the feelings of the Hortons was more important than spending the rest of his life in jail or going to the gallows. Late in the afternoon that same day, after spending a few more dollars from his diminishing supply of pocket money for a ticket on the steamer from Gravenhurst, Oscar was sitting in the study of the manse, trying to make James McCrum and the Huxleys understand why he was back in the village.

"Yesterday, when I was waiting to register at the University of Toronto, I just couldn't hand this over," Oscar said, holding up the envelope containing the money order. "The time has come for me to take control of my future and to pay my own way."

"I thought something like this would happen," said Mrs. Huxley, getting to her feet and leaving the room without looking back.

"I'll take that envelope, young man," said McCrum, snatching it from his hands. "If you ever return to these parts, don't forget to drop into the store to say hello. But right now I've got some work to do and have to go."

"I don't like this turn of events at all," said Reverend Huxley, "but it might do you good to take some time off before you resume your studies."

3

Later that night, Oscar was sitting in the doorway of a boxcar, his legs dangling outside, as the freight train he had hopped at Gravenhurst made its way through the northern Ontario night. He was surprised at how well his benefactors had accepted his change of plans. He had prepared mental notes to address all their anticipated objections, but no one had seemed to care. Maybe they thought he knew what he was doing and was big enough to take care of himself. Maybe they hadn't really forgiven him for drinking with Clem and helping him carry out his crazy act of revenge and didn't want anything to do with him anymore.

More likely, however, without intending to do so, he had released them from some sort of misguided sense of obligation, allowing them to forget him and get on with their lives.

At the same time, he knew he had been freed from the embrace of his benefactors and was able to resume his life where he had left it before his troubles started. He felt the cool, clean wind of early September on his face and imagined that he was thirteen again, after the wake held for Old Mary, looking out through a peephole scraped from the frost in the window of the train racing away from the Rama Indian Reserve toward Muskoka Wharf Station in the middle of the night. Looking up at the northern sky, Oscar remembered his intense joy he felt at being alive when he and Jacob, alone on Lake Muskoka under the Milky Way, paddled through the high waves to the Indian Camp. He remembered believing at that time that the soul of Old Mary, on its way to the Land of the Spirits over the Milky Way, was watching over him. He remembered singing "Shall We Gather at the River" at the top of his lungs and being comforted by the words.

Life had been so simple before the fire, when he was still a believer. He just wished his father was alive so that he could talk to him about God and the Creator and his plans to go to California.

❖

Early the next morning, the freight train slowed to a crawl and pulled into a siding at the Savant Lake railway station, deep in the northwestern Ontario bush. Jacob, he remembered, had once said his grandmother, Louisa, had taken the train from there when she went south to marry him in 1900. Savant Lake, he had also said, was just thirty miles away over a dirt road to the Osnaburgh Indian Reserve. He decided to visit the community to see if any members of Louisa's family were still alive with whom he could discuss his future. Later that afternoon, he knocked on the door of the first house he came to and asked the people within if they knew the Loon family, telling them the name of his great-grandmother was Betsy. To his surprise and immense pleasure, an old man led him to his great-grandmother who was in good health at the age of sixty-seven.

She cried out in fear when she saw him, thinking he was the ghost of her long-dead husband. After she recovered, she asked, "How is Louisa? I haven't heard from her since she got on the train to go south thirty- five years ago."

Oscar was forced to tell her she had been dead for decades. Betsy wept and said she should never have let her daughter go, but Jacob had seemed like such a responsible person. Later, during dinner, she asked Oscar why he had come to her reserve.

"I'm on my way to California," he said. "And I thought I'd drop in to visit with my relatives."

"You're looking for advice from an elder of your family you can trust, aren't you, Oscar?"

"I am, Granny. I'd like your guidance."

"Then first of all, tell me, why do you want to travel the world? Why don't you stay at home with your family on the reserve?"

"My mother doesn't want me, my grandfather is dead, and the white people who were taking care of me no longer want to have anything to do with me."

"There's more to this story than you've told me," Betsy said. And when Oscar, with much prodding, told her about setting the fire that killed his grandfather and precipitated the break with his mother and led some white people to feed, clothe, and educate him for five years, she laughed and laughed until the tears flowed down her cheeks. And when he described how he had drunk too much dandelion wine and helped Clem blow a great crater in the high-way and Dump Road to exact his revenge against the Port Carling village council, she found the strength to laugh some more.

"I once thought my destiny was to help our people, Granny. Do you think I can still do that if I go to California?"

"Your future will be decided by the Creator, no matter what you do or where you do it. And he wants you to be his trickster."

"What's a trickster, Granny?"

"Every so often, someone comes along and goes through life playing tricks on people," she said. "Sometimes they fool folks to take advantage of them; sometimes, it's to help them, like you did with Clem, but usually tricksters don't realize they've been deceiving people until it's too late. The Creator, the old people used to say, put tricksters on Mother Earth so he could have a good laugh in a sad world from time to time. So as you go through life, Oscar, and find yourself doing all sorts of strange things and getting into trouble, remember: the Creator is just having a good laugh at your expense."

PART 3

1948 TO 1958

Chapter 7

HOME FROM THE WAR

1

"I'll have a glass of draft beer, please," Oscar said, tossing a dime onto the bar after dropping into the Port Carling branch of the Royal Canadian Legion to look up old friends and to have a drink. He had graduated from the University of Toronto and was on his way to Ottawa to report for duty as a newly recruited foreign service officer in the Department of External Affairs, known in Canada and abroad simply as "the Department."

"Sorry, Chief, you can't drink here. We don't want the likes of you in the Legion. Besides, it's against the law to serve Indians. You being so well-educated and all that sort of thing, you shouldn't have to be told," said the bartender, a former teammate on the Port Carling hockey team in the old days.

"But I'm a veteran," Oscar said, "I served overseas. Don't I get any special treatment?"

"Even if you weren't an Indian, you'd still not be welcome.

So get out before I call the law. Go on down to the Indian Camp; your Indian buddies are all good customers of the bootleggers. They'll give you a drink if you ask them real nice."

Oscar looked around the room, seeking support from the dozen or more veterans of the two world wars, all of whom he knew from the time when he lived with the Huxleys. No one spoke up in his defence. Finally, an old soldier, someone who had fought with his father and Jacob at the Battle of Hill 70, said, "Why don't you just bugger off and let us drink our beer in peace."

Oscar stood at the bar staring at the old man until he looked away. He looked at the others, one after another, until they turned their backs on him and waited for him to leave.

"Call the cops if you want," Oscar then said to the bartender. "I'm not leaving until I get a beer."

"You always thought you were better than everyone else," the bartender said. "And you'd like nothing better than to have the cops come and throw you in jail. That way you could pretend to be a victim just like you did after the fire. Well, I'm not playing along with your game. You can stay as long as you want but I'm not serving you. You can watch the others drink."

Oscar picked up his money and left the Legion wondering why the veterans had decided to shun him. He went over the ridge to the Indian Camp, where a half-dozen veterans his age, friends from the old days when he was still a boy on the reserve, were drinking tea with their wives around a campfire while their children played in the water. They gave him the welcome he had expected to receive from the white veterans at the Legion and invited him to visit with them for a while.

"We haven't seen much of you in years," someone said. "Not since the Great Fire of 1930, when the white people took you in. Everyone figured your new friends told you to stay away."

"I did a lot of things in those days I regret to this day."

"Don't take it the wrong way; no one ever blamed you. You probably had no choice."

"I was just trying to survive after Jacob died."

"We're actually pretty proud of you. You seemed to land on your feet no matter what happened. You got a high-school education when none of us had that chance."

"But what happened back in 1935 when you were supposed to go to university to become a preacher?" someone else asked. "Did you have a falling out with the Huxleys?"

"Something like that," Oscar said "And it hadn't felt right to keep on accepting help from the white people when times were so tough for everyone. So I handed back the money they gave me for tuition, hopped a freight at Gravenhurst, went to California, and did whatever I could to earn a living."

Oscar thought it prudent not to mention that he had spent five wild years on the West Coast of the United States trying to find a world where he fit in. He had had his good and bad days. On the good ones, he managed to put aside his memories of the fire and his failed attempts to please his white benefactors at Port Carling. On the bad ones, he suffered through bouts of depression in which he relived the fire and the deaths of Jacob and Lily. Ultimately, he carved out a place for himself in a world of drifters, Mexican-American fieldworkers, down-and-out Okie and Arkie migrants fleeing the Dust Bowl of the Midwest, petty criminals on the fringes of society, and dispossessed American Indians. It was a world where he sometimes picked fruits and vegetables to make a little money, sometimes volunteered in soup kitchens, sometimes drank too much and passed out on the sidewalks, and sometimes slept in hobo jungles and flophouses. He even signed up on a whim with the Abraham Lincoln brigade to fight Falangist, Nazi, and Fascist troops slaughtering civilians in the Spanish Civil War, but the fighting ended before he finished his training.

In the end he found long-term employment. His chance came one night when he and a few of his friends went into San Diego after work to have some fun at a carnival. A barker was standing outside a tent, shouting out to the crowd that for only twenty-five cents they could watch an amateur boxer, Sven, "the Slovenly Swede," take on all comers.

"And if you want to fight him, big fellow," he said, looking at Oscar, "I'll wave the entrance fee and let you try your luck. The winning purse is ten bucks."

Oscar entered the ring and stripped off his shirt. Someone laced a set of boxing gloves on his hands and he was hit in the head before he could lift his arms. But he was big and strong in those days and in perfect shape from working in the fields. And although he had never had any professional training, he had played defence for the Port Carling hockey team and had never lost a fight. He poked, he jabbed, he danced around ring, and he flattened his opponent with one mighty punch, rendering him unfit to fight again. The carnival management offered Sven's job to Oscar, who became "Oscar the Killer Injun."

He made good money until he finally lost a fight and was fired. A member of the crowd who had been coming to see him perform in the ring then approached him. He told Oscar he was the owner of a bar on the waterfront and needed someone who knew how to use his fists to keep order at his place. And so for six nights a week for the next two years, Oscar threw drunken sailors from the nearby naval base out into the street when they became rowdy or belligerent.

The bar was also a hangout for prostitutes, who were always trying to get the sailors drunk and steal their money. Oscar did not approve of this type of behaviour, but in the interest of maintaining good relations with the girls, who were popular with the clientele, he looked the other way when they picked the pockets of their customers. He even came to enjoy their company, especially their ribald sense of humour, but in time he grew tired of them. He was still trying to cope with his depression and was almost happy when war broke out, since it gave him an excuse to return home and make a fresh start in the army.

❖

"And when the government declared war on Germany in September 1939," Oscar said, "I came back and joined the army, just like my father and grandfather did in the Great War."

At this point, the other veterans interrupted him to tell their own stories; how they too had joined up as soon as war had been declared, and how after their basic training at nearby Camp Borden, they had been among the first Canadian soldiers to be sent overseas to the giant Canadian base at Aldershot in England. Several had participated in the disastrous Canadian raid on Dieppe in German-occupied France in August 1942 and had been prisoners of war until the Allied victory in May 1945. Others had spent four years in England and fought their way ashore with the thousands of other Canadian soldiers in Normandy in June 1944 and participated in the major battles leading to Germany's surrender in May 1945. Several had been wounded. No one mentioned the ones who had not made it back.

"Since my father and grandfather had been in the 48th Highlanders," Oscar said, resuming his story during a lull in the conversation, "I joined the same outfit, and after basic training was sent overseas to Britain with my regiment in 1941. In 1943, I went ashore at Pachino with the others in the invasion of Sicily. After we chased the Germans across the Straits of Messina, we landed on the Adriatic coast and drove them out of southern Italy. And like a lot of you guys, I finished the war in May 1945 and came home to go to university. I graduated a few months ago and accepted a job in the Foreign Service."

"But why the Foreign Service?" the wife of one of the veterans, who had also known Oscar in the old days, asked. "Whatever made you decide to become a diplomat when you could have become anything you wanted — a preacher, a teacher, a doctor — something that would let you serve our people?"

"But being a foreign service officer will let me do that," said Oscar. "And not just the Native people of Canada, but other people just like ours everywhere."

Oscar did not say that the process of choosing the diplomatic life as a career had begun one night in Italy in the fall of 1943. He was by that time a sergeant in a company of men advancing in the pouring rain in single file up a steep goat trail behind enemy lines. They were on their way to seize the high ground and cut off the supply lines of a German unit blocking the forward movement of the Eighth Army up the Adriatic coast. It was so dark that each soldier had to hold the shoulder of the man in front of him to avoid stepping off the path and tumbling down the side of the hill and alerting the enemy. Suddenly, the column came to a halt and word was passed back through the ranks from the commanding officer at the head of the column: "Get the Chief! He's needed up front."

Oscar squeezed his way forward to where the commanding officer was waiting for him.

"The guys say there's a German guard post about fifty yards up ahead with a sentry standing in the doorway of a shed watching this trail. Your job is to take care of him as quietly as you can before he cries out. Otherwise his buddies will sound the alarm and we'll all be in the shit."

Oscar nodded, removed his pack, set down his rifle, took off the pouches filled with grenades and ammunition attached to the combat webbing around his chest, and set off up the hill armed only with his combat knife with its ten-inch blade. Moving ahead warily, he stopped every few yards to listen for sounds of the enemy and to peer ahead in an attempt to penetrate the veil of black pouring rain. Finally, he saw a glow and the outline of a face as the German soldier on watch sucked on his cigarette. Crouching down, his knife grasped firmly in his right hand, he waited patiently as the face of the German soldier, slumped against the door jamb of the goat shed, lit up periodically as he puffed away, unaware that Oscar was only two yards from him. When the soldier finished his cigarette and tossed it casually outside into the rain, Oscar stepped forward, placed a hand firmly over his mouth, wrapped an arm around his head, twisted it sharply, and slit his throat before he could raise the alarm. He dragged the dying man outside into the rain, took his place in the doorway, and listened to the breathing and snoring of other members of the German squad sleeping inside. After fixing in his mind their numbers and locations, he went back down the trail, quietly provided the password to the soldier on watch, and reported to the commanding officer who sent a team of soldiers with fixed bayonets to deal with the Germans asleep in the hut.

Later that night, hunched over and trembling from delayed shock in the waterlogged trench he and his comrades had dug on the brow of the hill they had just seized, Oscar was still savouring the praise he had received from his commanding officer for killing the sentry. It was not the first time he had carried out such a task and he liked to think he was chosen because he was the one who stepped forward when volunteers were needed for dangerous missions. He was the one who had distinguished himself by acts of bravery, leading the men of his platoon in attacks on enemy tanks and machine-gun nests as his regiment participated in the liberation of town after town from south to north in Italy. But these reasons aside, he had always welcomed the chance to show his solidarity with the men of the 48th Highlanders; they were his brothers-in-arms and his family, and family members helped each other, even at the risk to their lives.

The rain ended and Oscar got to his feet and looked out over the top of the trench at the tracer fire coming from the nearby German lines. As he waited for the enemy counterattack to begin, he remembered the soldier he had killed and the rush of adrenaline mixed with elation that had engulfed him when he slit his throat. He had felt the same way, he recalled, when he had set fire to the general store at Port Carling. A wave of shame swept over him, making him wish he had never been born. There was something despicable, perhaps evil within his soul that made him rejoice in the harm he inflicted on others. The depression that had plagued his life during his years in California was creeping back.

Afraid he wouldn't be able to participate in the coming engagement and be called a coward, he squeezed shut his eyes; he tried with all his might to fight off the mental anguish. He then remembered that years ago, when he was struggling to come to terms with his paralyzing fear of Jacob's shadow, he had realized that the gods were but figments of his imagination that he could drive away by an act of will. The guilt he had been carrying around with him for years, he saw, was something similar, a self-inflicted mental wound brought about by worrying about all the stupid things he had done in life. He needed to take control of himself. He needed to stop brooding on the past. If his mind threw up painful memories of the past, he would fight them by telling himself that that was then and now was now. He would remind himself that he had made a contribution to his country as a soldier that more than compensated for the errors of his youth. And should he survive the war, he would do even more for his people and his country.

Thus, at war's end, after two years of positive thinking, Oscar lined up with hundreds of other demobilized comrades-in-arms to register at the University of Toronto for his first year in the Humanities. This time, his fees and living costs were paid by the Canadian government under a program to help veterans reintegrate into society rather than by benefactors with their own agendas. This time, he felt at home studying with men and women his own age who had experienced war as he had, and who had no time for petty social snobbery. Three years of hard work then paid off when he graduated close to the top of his class and won the gold medal for International Relations and Modern History.

Faced with deciding what career path to follow, Oscar thought back to the evenings in the living room at the manse in Port Carling when Reverend Huxley had told stories about his journey back to Canada on the eve of the Great War. He remembered the hint of longing and lost opportunity in the reverend's voice when he talked about the sons of missionaries who had become diplomats and gone on to help solve the big international problems of the day. Inspired by his newfound confidence, Oscar decided to pursue the career denied to his benefactor, wrote the Foreign Service exams, and was rewarded by being offered a job as a junior foreign service officer. It had all seemed so easy.

But it was just as well for Oscar's morale that he did not know, and would never know, that he had almost been barred entry into the Foreign Service by the unchanged systemic prejudice against Indians. When the results of the country-wide examinations to select recruits came in, the selection board had been surprised to note that an Indian by the name of Oscar Wolf, a decorated war veteran and student in his final year at the University of Toronto, had scored high enough to merit entrance into the service. Such a thing had never happened before and they consulted the Department of Indian Affairs on the eligibility of Canada's First Peoples to become civil servants.

"Indians are indeed eligible," came back the Delphic reply, "as long as they are not Indians. The Indian agent on Mr. Wolf's reserve should obtain from him a sworn declaration that he renounces his status as an Indian as well as his right to live at any time at present or in future on his reserve. He will thus have the legal status of a real Canadian and be eligible to accept an appointment of Junior Foreign Service Officer in the Department of External Affairs."

The head of the selection board, afraid that Oscar might make a fuss, called on the undersecretary of state for External Affairs, the top-ranking official in the Department and a personal adviser to prime ministers going back for decades, to seek his views. The undersecretary, a man with a conscience who thought it was high time Canada began to practise at home the values it preached abroad at the United Nations, found a way around the regulations to let Oscar join the Department without renouncing his birthright.

2

When Oscar left the Indian Camp, he decided to call on the Huxleys, but when he went to the manse and knocked on the front door, nobody answered. However, the curtains parted and someone looked out at him. It was Mrs. Huxley and she did not look happy. The curtains closed, he heard footsteps retreating into the interior of the house, and then all was silent.

James McCrum greeted him coolly when Oscar dropped in to see him at the general store.

"What can I do for you today, sir," he said, glancing up from his desk as if he was meeting Oscar for the first time.

"Just thought I'd come in and say hello," Oscar said. "It's been a long time."

"Don't have time to talk, Oscar," he said, returning to his paperwork. "This is my busy season."

Oscar asked him about Clem.

"Oh, he's no better or worse than he's ever been," McCrum said, not looking up. "Spends his time drinking wine with that crazy mother of yours at his cabin on the Dump Road. He's still the village drunk."

Oscar was shocked at the changes in Clem when he went to see him. His face and eyes were yellow, his hair was sparse, his face was thin and haggard, and he limped when he walked.

"It's been so long, it's been so long since I seen you last," he said, wiping away with his hand the brown tobacco juice mixed with spittle that drooled from both sides of his mouth. "Why didn't you come back to see me, or at least write?" he asked, his eyes filling with drunken tears.

"I've got no excuse," Oscar said. "I should have. I was out west for years. I was in the army, and then at university."

"You Indian guys were always good soldiers, Oscar. I'm happy for you, I really am. But I've had a tough time, Oscar, since I seen you last. Honest to God, it's been tough. When I was in jail, they sold off all my pigs. I bought some more and when I couldn't keep up the fences around their pens and when they escaped they slapped the biggest jeezily fines on me you couldn't never believe, Oscar, again and again and again, until I used up all my money and had to go out of business. I looked for work but no one would give me a job, not even my own father. Then the war came along and our guys took so many German prisoners from downed planes and sinking ships in the Atlantic and Mediterranean there wasn't enough room in England to hold them. They turned the old TB sanatorium at Gravenhurst into a prisoner of war camp and started shipping them over here. They put out a call to Great War veterans to work as guards and I got taken on. But I felt sorry for those German fellows. I could tell they were homesick by just looking at them and so I started slipping them chewing tobacco to cheer them up, but I got caught and was fired. They said I was fraternizing with the enemy and that wasn't allowed.

"So they brought me to my knees, Oscar. I needed you, and you weren't there for me," he said, reaching for a tumbler of chokecherry wine. "The old ticker's been acting up and I use this as my medicine.

"Excuse me," he said, after taking a drink, "I should've offered you a glass."

"That's okay, Clem," Oscar said. "I'm not in the mood."

"Your mother and I have been drinking all day," Clem said, "and she's sleeping at the moment. She's a big-hearted woman, makes my meals and shares her pension cheques with me. Just wait a minute; maybe she'll want to say a few words to you."

Although he had seen her around the village often enough during his high school years, Oscar hadn't spoken to his mother since she had come to the door of the manse looking for him when he was living at the Huxleys. He hadn't wanted to have anything to do with her then, and he wanted nothing to do with her now.

"Don't go to the trouble, Clem, I'll see her some other time."

"But it's no trouble, Oscar. It's no trouble at all," Clem said, getting up and going into the bedroom.

"I'm sorry, Oscar," he said, coming back few minutes later. "She doesn't feel well enough to see you. Maybe she'll be her old self after when she's had a little more sleep. Why not come back later? Maybe have something to eat with us?"

"I'm sorry, Clem, but I can't stay. I've got to make it to Ottawa today. But before I go, do you have any idea why everyone around here is giving me the cold shoulder?"

"I think they know you started the fire, Oscar. Might even be my fault. I sometimes talk too much when I'm drunk. But they got no proof and they can't do nothing to you. They aren't about to make accusations they can't back up against a war hero."

Seeing Oscar's look of alarm, Clem blundered on.

"Actually, I'm not too sure what I said. It was after I got out of jail and found out they had sold off my pigs. I had a lot to drink and went downtown and told anyone who would listen that I had blown up their road because I wasn't going to let them push me around. I might have said that you had once done something like that. I might have mentioned that you torched the business section to pay back the villagers for stealing the land of your ancestors. The first thing I knew the constable was up at my cabin to take a statement. But I wouldn't make one. 'I say lots of wild things when I'm drinking and most of it's lies,' I said. And so they dropped the matter. I sure hope I haven't caused you any trouble."

"No, Clem, you didn't mean to cause me any harm. I've paid my debt to society through my service in the war and nobody has come after me in all these years."

"That's because they don't have a leg to stand on. The word of a drunk won't hold up in court. Your problem is the people around here don't like you as much as they used to. But that don't matter, because you still got me as a friend."

❖

Two weeks later, a letter addressed to Oscar Wolf, Foreign Service Officer, Department of External Affairs, Parliament Buildings, Ottawa, and postmarked Port Carling, Ontario, was sitting on Oscar's desk when he came to work in the morning.

Dear Oscar,

I am sorry I wasn't home when you dropped by the other day. Isabel said you came to the door and she didn't answer it. James McCrum has also told me that he sent you away when you went to see him. And everyone in the village is talking about how you were turned away at the Legion. You must feel hurt, but people who rejected you feel betrayed. I am sure you are aware by now that after you left Port Carling in the mid-thirties, a lot of rumours were spread about your possible connection to the Great Fire.

163

I want you to know that whether or not there is any truth to the rumours, I will stand by you. Everybody makes mistakes in life, sometimes big ones. And I for one made more than my share. I'm certainly not happy at the things I did in the war, killing Germans who were just doing their duty for their country. I hope God forgives me someday for I know I never will. It's something I'll carry to my grave.

Please come and see me sometime. We'll talk and it'll do the both of us a world of good.

Your Friend,
Lloyd Huxley

P.S. I understand that you have been accepted into the Department as a Junior Foreign Service Officer. I am so happy you managed to accomplish what I never managed to do.

Oscar read the letter and carefully filed it alongside the things most precious to him such as the medal for bravery in action His Majesty King George VI had given him at a ceremony at Buckingham Palace, a fading photograph clipped from the *Gravenhurst Weekly Gleaner* showing the Manido of the Lake against the setting sun on Lake Muskoka, and the pictures that used to hang on the wall of Jacob's house of his father and grandfather in their 48th Highlanders uniforms, saved from the trash by a neighbour back on the reserve and given to him after his mother had thrown them out.

Chapter 8

CLAIRE AND ROSA

1

Early in July 1948, Oscar reported for work with great hopes as a foreign service officer at the Parliamentary East Block headquarters of the Department of External Affairs. In Canada, he was Oscar Wolf, unclean, untouchable, outsider, Indian, forbidden by law by His Majesty's Government from drinking a beer at the Royal Canadian Legion at Port Carling and at every other legion post across Canada despite having served his country with distinction in the front lines in the army. But Oscar Wolf, member of Canada's Foreign Service, was someone who had gained entry entirely on his merits and was a respected insider among the architects of Canadian foreign policy when serving in Ottawa. And when posted abroad, he would be a distinguished diplomat representing all Canadians whatever the colour of their skin.

In the beginning, his expectations were fulfilled. He quickly adapted to the Department's quasi-military, quasi-ecclesiastic culture, especially the way its members behaved as if they had been initiated into holy orders. The recruits who entered with him that summer of 1948 were mainly former servicemen who had fought in the war and they welcomed Oscar, as a fellow veteran, into their ranks. Several of the senior officers treated him with some reserve, but they were graduates of Oxbridge in the 1920s and 1930s and they looked down on anyone who had not studied in the Old Country.

In September 1948, Oscar's staffing officer posted him to the Canadian mission to the United Nations in New York to assist Canada's representative on the United Nations Committee on Human Rights. Throughout the fall, he carried out research, wrote position papers, sent reports to Ottawa, lobbied other delegations, and to his great satisfaction was present on the historic day of December 10 when the General Assembly unanimously adopted the Universal Declaration of Human Rights. Spokesmen for the Canadian delegation told the press that acceptance by the international community of the declaration meant that victory over the evils of Nazism and Fascism was now being followed by triumph over injustice toward peoples and individuals. Soon the colonized peoples of the world would form countries of their own, which would take their places in the United Nations as members equal in status to the countries of the old imperial powers. But best of all, they claimed, the signatories to the declaration were bound to accord equal rights and freedoms to all their citizens, whatever their "race, colour, sex, language, religion, political or other opinion, national or social origin, property, birth or other status."

Oscar rejoiced. The Native peoples of Canada, he believed, would soon have the same rights as white Canadians. No longer would they be wards of the Crown. No longer would they be under the control of the Indian agent. No longer would they be deprived of the vote. No longer would they be forbidden to hire lawyers to defend their interests in court. No longer would

Indian women who married white men be expelled from their homes on reserves and be stripped of their identities as Treaty Indians. No longer would the police come and take away their children to residential schools. And he, Oscar Wolf, had played a part, however small as a foreign service officer, in bringing this new world into being.

But when Oscar returned to Canada in 1952 at the end of his posting, he found that nothing had been done to improve the lot of his people. The Indian agent still reigned supreme on the reserves and Native children were still being separated from their families and dragged off to residential schools. Elsewhere, the other countries that had signed the declaration in December 1948 with such great fanfare were likewise not doing anything to help their impoverished and marginalized peoples. In the United States, the Ku Klux Klan was still lynching blacks. In Latin America, white settlers were still stealing the land of the Indians. In Australia, the police were still tearing babies born to Aborigine mothers and white fathers from their families to be educated in special institutions away from their families. In South Africa, the ruling Afrikaner National Party was implementing its apartheid policy to keep blacks, coloureds, and Asians in a state of perpetual institutionalized servitude.

"Don't be discouraged," the undersecretary told Oscar when he went to see him. "Governments around the world, including Canada, are busy fighting the Cold War, and as soon as that's over, they'll get around to living up to their international human rights obligations. Just be patient."

2

In the meantime, Claire, who had played such an important part in Oscar's life back in the summer of 1935, was facing a crisis in her marital life. She had studied Art Appreciation and Home Economics at the University of Toronto and married Harold Winston White, a stockbroker from an old Toronto family, long-time friends of her parents. After the wedding, her husband's opinions became her opinions, his friends became her friends, and his passions for golf, tennis, and bridge became her passions. They had two children, a boy and a girl who were boarders at the same schools their parents had attended. In addition to doing volunteer work with wounded veterans at Sunnybrook Hospital, Claire was active in the University of Toronto Alumni Association and contributed used clothing, worn-out suitcases, chipped cups and saucers, discarded electrical appliances, and second-hand romance novels to the annual spring charity bazaar sale in her church's basement.

Claire and Harold had a home in Forest Hill close to the houses of their parents and a summer home on Millionaires' Row where they held their own Sunday brunches with family and friends and spent endless hours playing bridge and tennis at the nearby Muskoka Yacht Club. Every spring, they attended the races at Woodbine and Churchill Downs with friends who were horse breeders. Every winter, they spent six weeks at their home in a gated community in Grenada in the Eastern Caribbean where they hosted dinner parties under the stars with many of the same people who had estates on Millionaires' Row. They went marlin fishing from their yacht and were regular guests at Government House, where the British governor held parties for the British, American, and Canadian seasonal residents, as well for the members of the white expatriate community running the sugar plantations and nutmeg and mace farms. Occasionally, Claire and Harold passed people in the streets brandishing placards calling for freedom from British colonialism, but the governor assured them that independence would not happen in his lifetime.

Then, one day, Claire's husband of fifteen years noticed the beginning of wrinkles around his wife's eyes and upper lip and began to worry about his own mortality. Already forty-five, and wanting to be young again, he began having affairs with women twenty or twenty-five years younger than he was. Claire knew what he was doing but said nothing, not wishing to cause a scene, until one afternoon she returned home to find his clothes gone from his closet and a note on the dresser.

Dear Claire,

I have met someone else and I want you to give me a divorce. My lawyer will be in touch with yours.

Harold

Hoping Harold was just going through a temporary mid-life crisis and would soon be back, Claire did not give her consent. But Harold didn't come back, and she reluctantly settled for a divorce in exchange for custody of the children, the boy now aged ten and the girl twelve, ownership of the house in Forest Hill, possession of the Mercedes sedan, shared occupancy of the houses on Millionaires' Row and in Grenada, and fifty percent of his gross income.

It was then her turn to confront a mid-life crisis. The years had passed and she had little to show for them apart from a generous divorce settlement. Although she had custody of the children, they had their own circles of friends at their schools, rarely came home on the weekends, and when they did, always gave the impression they could hardly wait to leave. With the benefit of hindsight, it had probably not been a good idea to make them boarders when the school was only five hundred yards away. Certainly, when they were little, they hadn't wanted to live apart from their parents and there had been tears. But she had been a boarder and the experience had been good for her, or so she had once thought. Now she wasn't so certain.

Alone in a big house with no one to care for and nothing to do, she often thought of the idealism of her teenage years when she seemed to have more compassion in her soul. In those days, she had felt sorry for the thousands, maybe even tens of thousands of hungry people on the move in search of jobs or something to eat. She was strong in sciences in secondary school and had wanted to become a doctor and work for Dr. Albert Schweitzer who was running a hospital at Lambaréné on the Ogooué River in French colonial Africa. She had told her parents and they said they had no objection to her studying medicine. However, they didn't want her to work with Negros, especially in Africa where they lived in mud huts and had leprosy sores on their bodies. In her parents' opinion, Negros weren't much better than the Indians everyone saw asking for handouts and drinking cheap wine in downtown Toronto.

Maybe that was why she had been so attracted to Oscar back then. As an Indian, he represented the people she wanted to help. He was also the only dark-skinned person she had ever spoken to. And as she came to know him, she discovered he wasn't so different from the kids at her school. He laughed, he joked around, and he was easy to talk to. At the same time, he also wanted to help people and was planning to go to university to study to become a missionary to his people in the north. He even liked Chopin, her favourite composer, and seemed to have a crush on her.

Then she had this wild idea. She would invite Oscar to one of her family's Sunday brunches and they would see for themselves that dark-skinned people were as charming as anyone else. They would see in him what she saw in him — a decent human being who planned to make something of his life. But it had turned out badly. Her parents were so shocked when they saw him they covered up their embarrassment by treating him badly. And Oscar reacted by spilling his orange juice on the living room floor. Her furious parents refused to listen when she tried to tell them about his good qualities and ordered her to break off all contact with him. They must have thought there was more to the relationship than there really was. Taking the easy way out, Claire had dropped her plans to study medicine altogether. She then met and fell in love with Harold, and before she knew it, the years had gone by and she had nobody.

During all this time, she had never forgotten Oscar. She had tried to maintain a relationship in the beginning. She had telephoned him after the frigid reception she and her mother had given him at the general store, but didn't blame him for hanging up on her. The last time she had seen him was when they were both lining up to register for their first year courses at the University of Toronto, but he either hadn't heard her call his name or he had deliberately ignored her when he was leaving the building.

Some years later, just before she got married, in fact, she asked about him at the general store in Port Carling and was referred to Reverend Huxley, who told her that he had gone to California. Each summer, Claire made a point of attending at least one service at the Presbyterian church to pick up the latest news about him afterward over a cup of coffee. Early on, Reverend Huxley told her with a note of pride that Oscar had written to say he had left his job picking cherries and had found work in the entertainment business. Although Oscar had not spelled out exactly what that entailed, Reverend Huxley assumed that since he was living in California, and since Hollywood was in California, Oscar was now an actor playing Indian parts in the movies. As the years went by, Reverend Huxley let her know when Oscar joined the army, when he won medals for bravery, when he started university, and when he joined the Department.

With some hesitation, because she didn't know if Oscar was married or single or whether he was still upset with her for treating him so badly when they were teenagers, she looked up his name in the Ottawa telephone directory and called him. To her delight, he was glad to hear from her and they were soon seeing each other on a regular basis. Since Oscar only had a small one-bedroom apartment in Ottawa and a minuscule Foreign Service salary, she provided him airline tickets to fly to Toronto to spend the weekends with her at her place.

It did not take long for their intimate relationship, cut short in the summer of 1935, to resume. Her friends and family, however, were scandalized that she would take up with an Indian. She tried to include him in her social set but her friends stopped talking to her. Worried about what *their friends* might think, her children came up with excuses not to go home, and spent their weekends with their father and his new wife. The neighbours on Millionaires' Row did not include them in their Sunday brunches and the president of the Muskoka Yacht Club, someone Claire had known since she was a little girl, dropped by and told her as gently as possible that the members had asked him to tell her that they were not welcome to join their bridge games. When she took Oscar shopping at the general store in Port Carling, the villagers turned their backs on them. His friends and relatives at the Indian Camp, however, greeted them warmly when he took her to see them. Clem's welcome was just as enthusiastic when Oscar took her to meet him, and he kept Claire amused with his jokes and witticisms. She was puzzled, however, when Oscar's mother would not emerge from her bedroom to say hello.

In the summer of 1955, Oscar's staffing officer called him in and asked him if he would be interested in a posting to the embassy at Bogota, the capital of Colombia, three thousand miles away and nine thousand feet up on the windswept, rainy Alto Plano of the Andes.

"It would be a step up in your career," he said. "You would be one of only three first secretaries at the embassy, and if you do well, there will be greater things in store for you the next time around."

Oscar eagerly accepted the offer, but Claire was not happy when Oscar told her the news, especially since he hadn't consulted her before making his decision. She liked her house in Forest Hill; she enjoyed spending time at the homes whose ownership she shared with her former husband; and she didn't want to be so far away that she would hardly ever see her children, even if they were now avoiding her. And while she was glad she had connected with Oscar again, there were some things about him she didn't like. For example, when she took him to the opera, he was always asleep and snoring by the middle of the first act, whatever was on the program. When she persuaded him to accompany her to the running of the Queen's Plate at the Woodbine Race Track, he refused to wear a top hat and striped pants as required under the dress code, and she had been embarrassed when the race steward told Oscar he could not sit beside her in the VIP section. There were also times when he disturbed her sleep, crying out and laughing in the night, talking about his grandfather and someone named Lily.

Thus, while she was fond of Oscar, she certainly was not in love with him. And when he told her they should quickly get married to comply with the long-standing departmental edict that only married personnel could live together abroad, he mistook the look that came over her face as one of pure joy rather than one of utter panic as she contemplated spending the rest of her life supporting her husband in obscure diplomatic missions around the world and being treated as unpaid labour by the wives of ambassadors.

"You go ahead to Bogota and get things ready," she told him, desperately putting off the moment when she would have to inform him their relationship was over. And six months later, after mailing him letters every week saying how much she missed him and promising to join him when she had put her affairs in order, she sent him the following telegram:

> DEAR OSCAR. I am too much of a coward to tell you in person that I really do not want to get married. Not just to you but to anyone. I don't want to hurt you any more than I already have and so this is goodbye. CLAIRE.

3

In later years, Oscar would date the onset of his alcoholism, the start of his bizarre behaviour, and the collapse of his career to Claire's message rejecting him for the second time. When the messenger who had delivered the telegram left his office, Oscar turned his seat around to face the window and stared out at the low black clouds hanging over the bilious green eucalyptus trees on the hills behind the chancery for the rest of the afternoon. From time to time, the telephone rang, but he ignored it. Occasionally, someone knocked on his door and called out his name, but he remained lost in thought.

He saw himself back in the house on the reserve as a child of two or three again, unable to control his bowels, and his mother picking him up and shaking him, calling him a filthy animal, shoving him naked out into the snow and slamming shut the door behind him. Then he was six or seven years old at the Indian Camp. It was summer and his mother was chasing him, wielding a stick in her fist like a club, screaming at him to stop and take his punishment like a man after he upset her for some forgettable reason. Scared, he ran into the water to escape, and as he swam through the weeds away from the shore, he became entangled in what he at first thought was a thick piece of rope, but was terrified to discover was actually a long, thick black water snake. It thrust its triangular head and darting tongue at his face as it slithered and squirmed around his body trying to escape and he gave a great involuntary scream that he immediately regretted, because boys, he knew, were not supposed to be afraid of snakes. His mother called him a sissy for months afterward, never tiring of embarrassing him by telling the story to anyone who would listen. The blow to his pride, he remembered, had hurt him more than the beating she administered when he eventually went home to receive his punishment.

As for Claire, her message stung, but he harboured no strong feelings against her, certainly nothing to compare to the depths of the bitterness he felt toward his mother. But why couldn't she have just told him to his face that their relationship was over? He would have felt bad but would have soon recovered if she had made an effort to explain her reasons. This time he was older and less able to cope than when he was a resilient teenager back in 1935 and better able to shrug off the damage she had inflicted on his psyche.

That evening after work he went home, changed out of his suit, threw a poncho over his shoulders, went out into the dark, cold drizzle of Bogota's perpetual winter and flagged down a cruising taxi.

"*Llevarme a un bar,*" he told the driver. The driver laughed and drove him to a place he knew in a poor but tough part of the city where no diplomat would dare venture. A woman in a tight sweater and short skirt smoking a cigarette at the entrance greeted him like an old friend and offered to drink with him inside.

"*No, gracias,*" he said. But on seeing the look of disappointment that crossed her dark-brown, acne-scarred face, he reached into his pocket and gave her a twenty peso note. The woman smiled at him through broken teeth and pushed open the door for him. If this generous customer had problems and wanted to be left alone, she would respect his wishes.

Oscar stepped inside and waited a minute for his eyes to adjust to the bright lighting and low ceiling. The floor was wet and slippery from the water tracked in on the boots of customers, a duo was playing mournful Andean flute music, and there was a smell of damp ponchos, cheap perfume, and clogged toilet drains. With his dark skin, high cheek bones, and straight black hair, Oscar looked no different than the people who lived in the neighbourhood, and when he opened his mouth, he spoke with a local Spanish accent acquired from his live-in cook and maid. It was a perfect disguise. The waiter who led him to a table in the darkest corner of the room poured him, without asking, a shot of *aguardiente*, the cheap rotgut anise-flavoured sugarcane liquor favoured by the vast majority of poor Colombians out for a night on the town.

"*Quieres que deje esta contigo?*" he asked, and when Oscar nodded his agreement he left the bottle on the table and departed.

Oscar raised his glass and tossed its contents down his throat, only to gag on the raw drink and spit half of it out onto the floor. He refilled his glass and drank from it again, this time slowly, letting the alcohol dull his senses. Throughout the evening he continued to drink, determined to drive Claire from his mind through an act of will, just as he had with the existential issues of belief and redemption that had plagued his life in the aftermath of the fire. But the more he drank, the more he thought of her and the more he realized he would never forget her. The initial impact of her message had worn off, but he missed her more than ever.

One of the reasons he had so eagerly accepted the offer of a posting to Bogota, he now saw, was because he had expected Claire to ease his entry into the class-conscious society of Colombia. Now he would have to do it by himself, and wasn't sure he was up to the challenge. He had become dependent on her. He was shy, withdrawn, and found it hard to make friends. She was outgoing and mixed easily with people from all walks of life. She could discuss fashion trends, gourmet cooking, and travel destinations, subjects of little interest to him but which were of never-ending fascination for people in the diplomatic world he now inhabited. The Canadian staff at the embassy, while friendly enough, spent most of their spare time socializing with each other and playing tennis at the local country club while their children swam in a heated pool under the watchful eyes of a lifeguard.

An embassy colleague had once taken him to the club to meet the manager, helpfully explaining that the club rules denied membership to Negros and Indians unless they held diplomatic passports. While he was greeted and shown around courteously, he just couldn't see himself spending his free time at a club that excluded people like him.

By the time he finished his second bottle of *aguardiente*, Oscar was finding it hard to remain awake and decided to go home. He put a fistful of money on the table, rose to his feet, and stood for a moment until his head cleared enough to let him make his way to the exit without stumbling against the tables and chairs. Outside and looking for a taxi, he felt someone take hold of his arm. It was the prostitute he had met when he first entered the bar.

"Cuidado, no estas solo," she said, pointing at four men who had followed him outside, thinking he would be an easy mark despite his size. She hurried off as he turned and faced them. They pulled knives and surrounded him.

"Tu dinero, Indio, y rapido!" the one in charge told him, coming close with his knife in his hand.

Even with his senses impaired, Oscar was more than a match for his assailants. Reacting automatically, he drew on the hand-to-hand combat skills learned in the army to break the arm of his first attacker. He then turned on the others, kicking and beating them and driving them away. He calmed down on his way home in a taxi when he realized how close a call he had had. The police, had they been summoned to deal with the attempted robbery, would have submitted a report to the Colombian Ministry of Foreign Affairs, and it would have called in his ambassador to ask what his first secretary had been doing brawling with criminals in such an unsavoury place. He might well have been fired; he decided to stay out of bars in the future.

The next day, he bought half a dozen cases of *aguardiente* and began drinking in the mornings as soon as he woke up, in his office when no one was looking, and at home when he was alone in the evenings. He told himself that he could stop whenever he wanted, but he soon could not get through the day without his ration of alcohol. Fortunately, through trial and error, he learned that if he kept his consumption to one bottle a day, he could keep his depression at bay, remain steady on his feet, and not slur his words. Thus, although he began to display major errors in judgement at work, everyone assumed that was because he was basically incompetent, and no one suspected that it was because he had a drinking problem.

❖

One year into his posting, Pilar Lopez y Ordonez, the receptionist, rang Oscar in his office.

"There's someone here at the front desk to see you."

"Who is it? What does he want?"

"He wouldn't give his name. He just said he had something important to say to the Indian. I guess that means you."

Pilar was the twenty-two-year- old daughter of an old Colombian family whose ancestors had come with the first wave of Spanish colonists to New Granada in the sixteenth century to look for gold and to establish cattle ranches and coffee plantations. Despite the black roots of her straight, dyed blond hair, her piercing black eyes, and dark brown complexion, she would have been offended if anyone had insinuated that Indian blood ran in her veins. If asked, she would have said that she had nothing against *los indios*, as she and members of her class disdainfully called Indians, as long as they knew their place: and their place was working for pittances seven days a week and twelve months each year as maids and cooks for the people of her social station. Another place for them, one she and her friends never discussed but tacitly accepted, was that of serving as unwilling sexual partners for their younger brothers, breaking them in, so to speak, before they married respectable women and founded families of their own.

From the day of Oscar's arrival at the embassy, Pilar hadn't liked him because he was *un indio*, even if a Canadian one. She had naturally treated him with the same indifference and disdain she reserved for *los indios* in the family home, but wasn't worried about being fired. She didn't need her job, or any job for that matter; her family had plenty of money, and she had become a receptionist only to fill in time at a prestigious embassy until she met the right person and got married.

"He's over there," she said to Oscar when he went to the reception area, pointing at a sunburned, full-bearded man who was reading an out-of-date copy of the *Globe and Mail*. A few minutes later, in Oscar's office, the visitor identified himself as Luigi Ponti, a doctoral student in anthropology from the University of Verona conducting research on the Cuiva Indians of the tropical rainforest on the Meta River, close to the border with Venezuela. Death squads, he said, hired by ranchers who wanted to drive away the Indians in order to graze cattle on their lands, had moved into the area, burning their villages and shooting them on sight. He had gone to the police but they refused to act. He had spoken to Colombian bureaucrats, called on politicians of all political parties and even approached the newspapers.

"But nobody wants to do anything about it; they all say they're afraid of the big landowners and their hired thugs. But I think the real reason is the governing class quietly supports the death squads. Getting rid of the Indians would open up vast areas of the country and be good for national development. I'm now making the rounds of the embassies trying to get them to take an interest in what's going on down there. So far, I've been to see the Americans, the French, the British, and the Dutch. They all told me that nobody back in their capitals is interested in the fate of a few primitive Indians in the jungles of Latin America. Their publics are all out of compassion. The horrors of the war burned them out."

"And so you've come to me because someone told you I was an Indian?" Oscar asked, pouring shots of *aguardiente* for his guest and for himself.

"That's right," Luigi said, drinking to Oscar's health. "I took a chance that you might be interested in the fate of your brothers down here."

❖

"I'd like to help, Oscar, honest to God I would," said Georges Leroux, Canada's ambassador to Colombia.

The ambassador had grown up in the 1920s and 1930s in Mexico City, where his father was an expatriate businessman, and had attended a school for the children of rich foreigners and upper class Mexicans. On his way to and from school each day, he could not help but see the poorly dressed, underfed, suffering people, especially the Indians, who came into the city each day in search of work.

"You have lots of money," he told his father, "why don't give some of it to the poor?"

"I'd like to help, son," his father had said, "honest to God I really would, but the problem is far too great for any one person to solve."

Georges hoped his father was wrong, and after graduation from McGill University in the late 1930s, he joined the

Department hoping to make the world a better place. However, his staffing officer posted him to the Canadian embassy in Buenos Aires to spend the war as an assistant to the Canadian trade commissioner. With the resumption of peace in 1945, Georges asked to be sent to the Canadian mission to the United Nations to work on human rights issues, but he had demonstrated such a flair for trade promotion in Argentina that the Department denied his request and sent him as trade commissioner to the Canadian embassy in Havana, Cuba.

Canada's ambassador in Havana, however, was a unilingual Anglophone who neither spoke nor had any interest in learning to speak Spanish. And since the great majority of Cubans did not know English, or if they did, preferred to speak their own language with their foreign contacts, the circle of contacts of the head of post was confined to the American and British ambassadors and members of the overseas Canadian community. Georges, who spoke Spanish like a native Cuban, thus became responsible for developing and maintaining links with members of Cuba's government and power elite.

The Department quickly promoted him to the rank of deputy ambassador to reflect his new duties and moved him into a fully furnished three-bedroom, four-bathroom house with extensive gardens filled with fragrant yellow and white flowering frangipani plants and chirping crickets. A cook, maid, and gardener, who lived in staff quarters on the grounds discreetly out of sight of the main house, prepared his meals, washed and ironed his clothes, and cut the grass, tended the gardens, and brought him gin and tonic cocktails with snacks whenever he rang a little bell. He became accustomed to cha-cha-cha music and white-tie dinner parties in the hot and humid night air around swimming pools under giant royal palm trees. Profiteroles stuffed with vanilla ice cream and covered in hot chocolate sauce became his dessert of choice. Dom Perignon champagne, Chambertin burgundy, and Château d'Yquem sauterne, purchased at the local diplomatic duty-free shops, became his favourite wines. He relished the atmosphere of the casinos frequented by mobsters from Miami and corrupt government officials and their high-priced call girls. Each time a high roller won or lost millions at the throw of the dice, and whenever bombs placed by revolutionaries trying to overthrow the government exploded nearby, an addictive thrill of excitement, a sense that he was living life on the edge, ran through his body.

Georges decided that he wanted to spend the rest of his career in Latin American capitals like the Havana of the late 1940s and set aside his youthful enthusiasm for making the world a better place. And because he proved to be so good at promoting trade and making friends with the people who counted in Latin American society, the Department acceded to his desire, and in no time at all he rose to become an ambassador. His son, who attended local private schools in the countries of his service, and who was deeply concerned at the sight of so many beggars on the streets, sometimes asked his father why he never did anything to help the poor, but he never received a satisfactory answer.

❖

"The Spaniards and then the Colombians have been slaughtering Indians in this country for centuries," Ambassador Leroux said, continuing to lecture Oscar, "and they'll keep on slaughtering them until the last one is dead. When they're not killing Indians, they're killing each other. In the last three years they've murdered a half-million of their own people in some of the most godawful ways. We don't know what makes these people tick. They're crazy. I think they like killing people. Outsiders shouldn't get involved. It wouldn't do any good if we did."

"But we're living in the twentieth century," Oscar said. "Canadians helped draft the United Nations Charter and signed the Universal Declaration of Human Rights. Surely we should speak out when we see governments standing by and doing nothing when their Indians are being killed."

"Oscar, I feel like I'm talking to my son. You were a soldier. You've seen the Nazi death camps, I presume. You know what man is capable of doing. And yet you're more than a little naïve. We signed those human rights declarations just for show, just to make us feel better for treating your people, and all the others in Canada who have no power, the way we do, just to make us look good internationally. The Indians will remain at the bottom of the heap for my lifetime at least. I shouldn't have to tell you all this."

"What if I was to go with this anthropologist and see what's going on for myself and send a report to Ottawa?"

"What do you think we would do even if you prove the allegations are true?" asked the ambassador, who always associated himself with the Canadian government in his pronouncements. "We would do nothing. And we wouldn't do anything if we could. In embassies in these places in the middle of nowhere, we don't care about Indians. What we care about down here is selling asbestos, mining equipment, diesel generators, automobiles, tractors, trucks, bagged flour, and shiploads of beans, anything at all to make a buck and keep Canadians working. When we can't sell our goods fair and square, we do like our competitors and bribe the hell out of the corrupt bastards in charge to get the deals, even if they just pass on the increased costs to the poor. And when you get right down to it, there's no real difference between bribing people and killing Indians except the amount of evil involved. We all agreed to get our hands dirty, whether we knew it or not, when we joined the government. We're all Indian killers, Oscar, even you."

Overcome by his admiration of his own eloquence, Georges took Oscar by the hand, squeezed it, and said, "But go for it, Oscar. Go find out what those bastards are really doing, and we'll see what we can do to help!"

❖

With his backpack stocked with bottles of *aguardiente*, Oscar travelled with Luigi by bus, communal taxi, DC-3 aircraft, and canoe to the place of refuge of the Cuiva Indians, hidden from the death squads in the jungle fringe along the wide, slow-moving Meta River.

In his alcohol-induced daze, Oscar felt as if he had entered the world of the ancestors as described to him by Old Mary during the evenings in her house around the kitchen table when he was a boy. In the mornings, he stripped naked and swam with the others in the deep, sheltered warm waters of a lagoon. In the evenings, he shared the meals of turtle eggs, catfish, crocodile, and monkey meat, prepared by the women over an open fire. Later on, before retiring to his hammock, he sat down on the riverbank and listened, as Luigi interpreted for him, to the murmur of the people discussing the events of the day and pointing up at the stars and repeating the legends passed down to them by their ancestors over the millennia.

One morning, as he ate his breakfast, he saw a young woman looking at him. She was over six feet tall, with wide hips, large breasts, smooth chocolate-brown skin, and thick, straight black hair that fell down to her waist. Never before had he seen a woman with such a beautiful smile. Never before had he been so attracted to someone at first sight. It never occurred to him that her natural beauty had been enhanced by the *aguardiente* he had just drunk. He smiled at her and she looked away. She looked at him, he smiled back at her and she looked away. It became a game. One night, she came unbidden and joined him in his hammock. And throughout their night of lovemaking, because he couldn't pronounce her name, he called her his little Rosa.

"You shouldn't have done that," Luigi told him when he saw them together. "What if your Rosa gets pregnant? You won't be here to take care of her and no man will want her. I should have warned you. Never sleep with the Indians. It's the golden rule of anthropology. And by the way, in the language of her people, her name is Morning Star."

"But I'm Indian, too, Luigi," Oscar said. "I'm exempt from that rule. As far as I'm concerned, she'll always be my little Rosa."

When the visitors left to return to Bogota, Rosa and Oscar both cried. Two months later, Luigi came to the embassy accompanied by Rosa and asked for Oscar.

"Your friend is back and he's not alone," Pilar informed him.

Oscar could scarcely contain his pleasure at seeing Rosa again, even though she spoke only Cuiva and could only communicate with him by sign language. He had thought of her often during their weeks of separation, remembering the heat of the night on the bank of the Meta River and their two bodies thrashing around in his hammock as the posts supporting the five hundred pounds of their combined weight creaked and groaned. He would sometimes see her in his dreams swimming naked in the river. At other times in his imagination he would picture her dressed in the latest designer gown, the most elegant woman in the room, swinging her hips and smiling that captivating smile of hers as she strutted with supreme effortless panache down the runway of a famous Parisian fashion house on the Faubourg Saint-Honoré as the crowd clapped their hands in appreciation. And although Rosa now looked at him as if he were a complete stranger, he was certain she had missed him as much as he had missed her.

"I told you you'd get into trouble when you slept with Rosa," Luigi said, after Oscar escorted his guests back to his office. "Her family says she's pregnant and is now your responsibility."

Oscar immediately asked Luigi to tell her he wanted to marry her.

"You don't have to do that," Luigi said. "You can take her to a convent, make a donation, and after the baby is born, the nuns will find someone to take it. They'll give Rosa Spanish lessons, teach her to cook simple meals, scrub floors, and wash clothes, and then they'll get her a job as a maid or cook with a rich Bogota family. She won't be as happy as she'd be if she was living with her family back on the river, but she'll have a roof over her head and be fed."

Oscar wouldn't hear of it. No child of his would be put up for adoption. What if the adoptive parents didn't love the baby? What if they were just looking for unpaid labour? What if they were to beat the child? What if they were like Pilar and were prejudiced against Indians? No child of his would grow up to be as unloved as he had been. And there was Rosa, his darling little Rosa. She would not spend the rest of her life as a poorly paid servant when she could be the wife of a distinguished Canadian diplomat. He loved her, or at least he thought he did. She would never lead him on and dump him as Claire had done. She was a pure and noble Indian, just like he was, and he wanted more than anything else to spend the rest of his life with her.

When they heard the news, Oscar's Canadian colleagues told him he was making a big mistake, Pilar had trouble keeping from sneering, and Ambassador Leroux was offended.

"You're out of your mind. You just can't wander off into the jungle, pick out a mate, and bring her back to marry as if you were some sort of caveman. Civilized people don't do things like that. Members of the Department don't behave like that!"

Ambassador Leroux, Oscar thought, was just upset because he had neglected to investigate the reports of death squad activities despite his lengthy absence on official business in the Orinoco River Basin. Oscar was sure he would come around after he had thought about the matter for a few days. But Ambassador Leroux did not come around. He sent a telegram to the under-secretary to give him the news and to recommend that Oscar be returned to Canada and fired.

As the ambassador waited anxiously for an answer, the Bogota newspapers covered the story in all its salacious details. Columnists, tipped off by Pilar, who had learned that Rosa was pregnant, provided lurid accounts of how Oscar had left the capital for the Orinoco River Basin to save the Indians from extermination at the hands of death squads; how swimming among the piranhas, he had met and seduced a buxom Indian maiden; how he had returned to Bogota leaving his newfound love alone and forlorn in her thatched hut; how two months later she arrived pregnant at the door of the Canadian embassy with a ragged, long-haired student from the University of Verona; how the distinguished first secretary of the Canadian embassy to the Republic of Colombia intended to wed his sweetheart in holy matrimony; how Ambassador Leroux was beside himself with rage; and how the Canadian embassy was now the laughing stock of the entire diplomatic corps.

The telegram from the undersecretary, when it finally arrived, was not to Ambassador Leroux's liking. The message, copied to the prime minister, the minister of Indian affairs, the minister of national defence, the minister of citizenship, and the RCMP Security Service, took some time to get to the point.

> Acknowledge receipt of your message of 1 September. Am personally acquainted with Wolf and am sorry to hear of his troubles. Have consulted within Department with Latin American Division, Legal Division, United Nations Division, Communication Division, Information Division, Protocol Division and Defence Relations Division, and outside Department with Department of the Prime Minister, Department of Indian Affairs, Department of Veterans Affairs, Department of Justice, Department of Revenue,

Department of the Solicitor General, Department of Federal-Provincial Relations and the Royal Canadian Mounted Police to find solution. There is consensus matter is delicate and everyone stresses importance in exercising great prudence in handling bearing in mind Wolf is only Indian officer in Department and for that matter in entire Canadian civil service. For almost one hundred years, Canadian governments have been trying to prepare Indians to abandon their savage customs and to adopt civilized ways of white man. If all goes according to plan, it is expected that within decade or two, Indians will be given privilege of voting in elections as well as some legal rights presently reserved for white people. Thus would not want, repeat would not want, Wolf to leave Civil Service. He is war hero and example of what governments have been attempting for generations to accomplish with Indians. Worse, if fired because he wishes to marry Indian woman, even Colombian Indian woman, Indian people of Canada and churches would be irritated.

Please provide all necessary assistance to Wolf with his marriage plans, including making representations to Colombia to expedite paperwork and closing embassy day of wedding. Staff are to attend ceremony and to give wedding presents. Extend my personal best wishes to the happy couple and in due course facilitate return of Wolf and his bride to Canada.

The Undersecretary of State for External Affairs, Ottawa, Ontario, Canada